Later Days at Highbury

Also by Joan Austen-Leigh

Stephanie
Stephanie at War
A Visit to Highbury

PLAYS (Joan Mason Hurley)

Our Own Particular Jane
Canadian One Act Plays for Women
Four Canadian One Act Plays
Women and Love
Women's Work

Later Days at Highbury

Joan Austen-Leigh

St. Martin's Press
New York

Library of Congress Cataloging-in-Publication Data

Austen-Leigh, Joan.
    Later days at Highbury / by Joan Austen-Leigh.
       p.   cm.
    ISBN 0–312–14642–6
    I. Title.
  PR9199.3.A912L38   1996
  813'.54—dc20   96–24520
                                                                    CIP

First Edition: November 1996

10 9 8 7 6 5 4 3 2 1

To
my sister, Valerie Peyman
great-great-great-niece
of
Jane Austen

Apologia

Jane Austen once told a niece who wanted her to write a letter as from Georgiana Darcy that she was "not at all sure" what sort of letter Georgiana would write. By the same token I am not at all sure what Emma and Mr. Knightley might say to each other when they are alone and settled at Donwell. I prefer to take no liberties; I do not intrude. I leave them to their well-earned privacy and peace.

But the temptation to visit Highbury once more I find irresistible. I have taken Jane Austen's mistress of a school, Mrs. Goddard, who does not speak a single word in *Emma*, as the central character of my book, included some of JA's other characters in minor roles and added a number of people of my own.

I am a little dubious of sequels, as such. Therefore, I have tried to write not so much a sequel, as a continuing history of that beloved English village, Highbury.

—J A-L

She was very fond of Emma, but did not reckon on her being a general favourite. . . . She would, if asked, tell us many little particulars about the subsequent career of some of her people. In this traditionary way we learned that . . . Mr. Woodhouse survived his daughter's marriage, and kept her and Mr. Knightley from settling at Donwell, about two years.

—J. E. Austen-Leigh
Memoir of Jane Austen

"Mrs. Goddard was the mistress of a School—not of a seminary, or an establishment, or any thing which professed, in long sentences of refined nonsense, to combine liberal acquirements with elegant morality upon new principles and new systems—and where young ladies for enormous pay might be screwed out of health and into vanity—but a real, honest, old-fashioned Boarding-school, where a reasonable quantity of accomplishments were sold at a reasonable price, and where girls might be sent to be out of the way and scramble themselves into a little education, without any danger of coming back prodigies. Mrs. Goddard's school was in high repute—and very deservedly; for Highbury was reckoned a particularly healthy spot: she had an ample house and garden, gave the children plenty of wholesome food, let them run about a great deal in the summer, and in winter dressed their chilblains with her own hands. It was no wonder that a train of twenty young couple now walked after her to church. She was a plain, motherly kind of woman, who had worked hard in her youth, and now thought herself entitled to the occasional holiday of a tea-visit; and having formerly owed much to Mr. Woodhouse's kindness, felt his particular claim on her to leave her neat parlour hung round with fancy-work whenever she could, and win or lose a few sixpences by his fireside."

—from *Emma*

Cast of Characters

Sophy Adams, *niece of Mr. Pinkney, pupil at the seminary of Madame Dubois*

Paddy O'Ryan, *(Robert) footman at the seminary*

Mr. John Knightley, *formerly of Highbury*

Isabella Knightley, *his wife,* (née *Woodhouse*) *sister to Emma in Highbury*

the Rev. Philip Elton, *former vicar of Highbury*

Augusta Elton, *his wife*

Mr. Wingfield, *apothecary*

AT ENSCOMBE IN YORKSHIRE

Frank Churchill, *son of Mr. Weston in Highbury*

Jane, *his wife,* née *Fairfax, niece of Miss Bates*

AT MAPLE GROVE, BRISTOL

Selina Suckling, *sister of Mrs. Elton*

Mr. Suckling, *her husband*

Later Days
at Highbury

Letter 1

(From Mrs. Goddard to Mrs. Pinkney)

The School
Highbury
Monday 16th September 1816

My dear Charlotte,

A new school year has begun and I have no business to be writing to you when there are many other matters that require my attention. But I cannot resist doing so, since I flatter myself that you take an interest in the affairs of Highbury and I have two rather particular pieces of intelligence to communicate. One is joyful, the other sad.

I will start by posing a question. Can you guess whom I met this morning? I am sure you cannot. I was on my way to Ford's when I descried Emma Knightley passing along the Donwell road in her carriage. At precisely the same moment she noticed me and called out to James to stop the horses. She has been keeping very much to herself since her father died, and I have not actually spoken to her for some weeks. As I approached she let down her window and asked me in a very friendly manner how I did.

That was this morning. It has been a busy day and I trust I may finish this before four o'clock dinner, then John can run over to the post office and you will receive it tomorrow.

My sad news is that last night poor old Mrs. Bates died. It was not altogether unexpected. After Mr. Woodhouse had gone Mrs. Perry told me that Mr. Perry surmised Mrs. Bates would not last two months. And so it has proved to be. Poor dear old lady.

Ah, a knock! Miss Richardson at my parlour door.

1

Later: You may hardly credit it, my dear Charlotte, but we are so full this term that the girls' trunks, usually stored in the attics, are sufficiently numerous that they have overflowed the space allotted to them. Miss Richardson was at her wits' end. "Mrs. Goddard," said she, "however can one dispose of *trunks?* They are so *big.*" I suggested we consult John. John can always think of something. He came. He scratched his head. He pondered. He proposed the stables. Of course! Since we have no horses, this extra building, where he himself sleeps, is quite at our disposal. Yet I never thought of it! I can see John from my window now, trundling back and forth with a laden wheelbarrow.

Having settled that, and one or two other trifling matters, I am able to resume. I was telling you about Mrs. Bates. Once our card parties at Hartfield were no more, she seemed to lose all heart, and has been declining gently away, giving in her death as little trouble as ever she did in life. It is as well that just now I have not leisure to dwell on these sad events, but when winter comes and I sit alone by my fire I shall not cease to remember my two dear old friends and the happy times we shared together.

I wrote a letter of condolence to Miss Bates this morning before breakfast, and sent John round with it together with a basket containing a nice cold roast chicken and some apple turnovers that Sarah had made. Then after breakfast I set off for Ford's to place my usual order for flannel petticoats. At least that was the reason I gave Miss Nash, whom I imagined was raising an eyebrow when she saw me walking out with my bonnet on. I felt a little deceitful. Not that the petticoats have not to be ordered. Indeed, they must. You would hardly believe, my dear Charlotte, how many parents fail to furnish their daughters with this most indispensable item. You will say that the girls ought to make their own, as we used to do. But I have long since learned that it is useless to expect it. They would never be ready before the snow flies. Since winter and chilblains and everything of that sort is some weeks off, I cannot pretend that this visit to Ford's was precisely urgent business. As you have guessed,

2

it was an excuse to go out for I was anxious to hear the news.

It was a most happy chance that I should encounter Emma Knightley, for besides hearing about Mrs. Bates, which was my chief concern, I also learned that she was actually on her way to Donwell Abbey to give instructions to Mrs. Hodges. It is two months since Mr. Woodhouse died and at last they are planning to move. Emma volunteered that she had not felt quite equal to doing so until now and that Mr. Knightley had been very sympathetic and understanding in the matter. He, of course, was to have accompanied her today, but having offered to take charge of the funeral arrangements he could not be spared. Mrs. Hodges, however, was so eagerly anticipating them that it was resolved the good woman should not be disappointed and Emma should proceed alone. I expect I have mentioned that Mrs. Hodges has been living at the Abbey these two years on board wages with the furniture shrouded in dust sheets. One does not need a great imagination to comprehend her joy at the prospect of the return of her master.

Emma seemed in no hurry to be off to what, I suppose, might be for her a somewhat difficult interview. So while the horses snorted and tossed their heads, and James cast reproachful glances over his shoulder at me (which I could see, but which Emma could not) she continued our conversation. The date of Mrs. Bates's funeral depends on the arrival of Jane and Frank Churchill. An express was sent to Enscombe last night and it is concluded that they could possibly appear so soon as the day after tomorrow—if they leave at once and if they use four horses. They will stay at Randalls and Mrs Weston has invited Miss Bates to join them there afterwards. (The service will be taken by our new young vicar, Mr. Rutherford. I did tell you, did I not, that the Eltons have gone?) The invitation to Miss Bates surprised me a little. I have never thought of Mrs. Weston and Miss Bates as *intimate*, aside from the circumstance that the son of Mr. Weston is married to the niece of Miss Bates. Undoubtedly the kindest intentions have inspired this arrangement, and being at Randalls will certainly enable Miss Bates to

3

see as much as possible of her beloved niece during their visit. Yet I cannot help but feel she would have preferred to remain where she was and be at liberty to receive her friends at home. It must be a contrivance, too, on the part of Mrs. Weston, since one knows she has but two spare bedrooms. I conclude the Churchill servants will put up at the Crown.

While I had the chance, I made a point of telling Mrs. Knightley how much Mrs. Bates, Miss Bates and myself had appreciated her continuing after her marriage to invite us to Hartfield to play cards with her father. I observed that it had given much pleasure to four old people (now do not chide me, I pray, for calling myself old). This is nothing less than the truth, dear Charlotte, and she made a gracious reply. Yet at the same time, *entre nous*, I imagine that our presence did give her and Mr. Knightley a few moments' respite in their constant administrations to Mr. Woodhouse. He could not be left alone in a room, you know, for as much as five minutes at a time.

In fact, Mrs. Perry once admitted to me in confidence that whenever Mr. Perry had a disengaged hour he would call in at Hartfield simply in order to give them an opportunity to stroll in the shrubbery or to talk privately together. He made no charge for these visits, and I am happy to say he has been rewarded. I understand Mr. Woodhouse remembered him in his will.

As for Mr. Knightley, in the opinion of Highbury, his forbearance has been beyond anything. Having ever since his marriage lived as a guest in his father-in-law's house, at last he can return home with a good conscience taking his wife and child with him. So you see, my dear Charlotte, what changes are afoot in our quiet little Highbury.

Since I had heard from Emma everything I wanted to know and a great deal more, besides, I concluded my place was at school, and if asked by Miss Nash I would have to confess that I'd postponed the ordering of the petticoats.

It is fortunate I came back when I did. I found the kitchen in an uproar. The baker had not delivered the increased number of loaves Sarah had ordered and very sharp words indeed were being exchanged. I had to smooth many ruffled feathers before peace was restored. Then the music master came complaining that the pianofortes had not been tuned, and Miss Prince informed me with some asperity that there was a shortage of slates. On top of all this two or three of the new girls claimed to be homesick. So at midday I had them into my parlour and administered hot chocolate and cake and comforting words until they were ready to return quite cheerfully to their schoolfellows.

There is the dinner bell!

Before I seal my letter, I must again observe that it is high time your sweet little Edward was introduced to his fond aunt and godmother. Would Mr. Pinkney consider your spending the Christmas in Highbury, do you think? It is not too soon to plan and I long to see for myself that your treasure's hair is as fair and his eyes as blue as you describe.

Ever your most affectionate sister,
Mary Goddard

Letter 2

(From Mrs. Pinkney to Mrs. Goddard)

Hans Place
London
Wednesday 18 September 1816

My dear Mary,

De mortuis nil nisi bonum. Do you remember how often our father used to quote that? It is one of the few Latin tags that sticks in my memory. I realize how fond you were of Mr. Woodhouse and Mrs. Bates, but surely, *surely*, their deaths cannot be occasion for *very* deep mourning. For Emma and Miss Bates it is positively a liberation.

Invitations to Hartfield I know you welcomed, and I am sorry for your sake that they have come to an end. But how different are your tastes from mine! Wild horses could not drag me to a house where I was offered gruel, while delicious food was presented only to be swept away because my host fancied it undercooked! A fricassee of sweetbreads and asparagus, denied to Mrs. Bates, I particularly remember your mentioning.

To *you*, Mr. Woodhouse was a beloved old pet, but to *me* he was a spoiled child. Imagine, a grown man, unable to stay in a room alone! It is a wonder Emma and Mr. Knightley ever managed to conceive a child. But I suppose he must not have followed them into the bedroom. Oh dear! Mary, you are not going to like that remark. But I will not ruin my page by scratching it out, for it is the truth.

Well, well, who will occupy Hartfield, I wonder? And what is to become of Miss Bates? We suppose her income will be very materially reduced? Mr. Pinkney conjectures that she will be obliged to accept charity at Enscombe. I say "obliged" is not at all the right word. *I* think she will be overjoyed at the prospect of being under the same roof as that perfect paragon and prig, her niece, Jane Fairfax. The person I pity is Frank Churchill. How will he bear it?

You are right, my dear Mary, it is indeed too long since we last visited Highbury. I read your letter aloud to Mr. Pinkney. He was vastly entertained by your speaking of your desire to see your nephew.

"Pray, tell your sister," said he, "that it is all very well for her to talk of being a fond aunt, but I recall very clearly that when Edward was born she was quite vexed. I distinctly remember her words: 'I was hoping for a girl, then she could come to my school. Of what use is a boy? I do not know how to talk to boys.'"

"I remember that, too," I said, "but when she meets Edward she will be charmed."

"Of course," said he. "And I know how anxious you are to see your sister, and to show off our treasure. But I would rather he was not exposed to the hazards of the road."

"Ah, your precious son!" said I, for he is absurdly protective of Edward.

"My dear," said he, "consider that the child is four months short of being two. I think he should be at least three, if not four years old before we attempt such a thing."

"It is not exactly a fearsome journey," said I. "Frank Churchill rode from Highbury to London and back simply to have his hair cut. You remember Mary telling us that?"

"Only it was really to buy a piano," said he, "and is nothing to the purpose."

"My dear Mr. Pinkney, you must take care or you will become as big a fusspot as Mr. Woodhouse."

"Only I shall never be persuaded to eat gruel."

"Nobody is proposing gruel, only a visit to Highbury. The way you go on, one would think Edward was heir to the throne, at least."

"Indeed," said he.

"Whatever do you mean by 'indeed'?" said I, quite vexed. "You must know it is an affliction of elderly parents to fancy their own child the most important in the kingdom."

"My love, you are mistaken," said he earnestly, "How could you think so ill of me? Not in the kingdom, but in the whole wide world."

I had to laugh. Dear, silly man. He has no shame. Almost every day he thanks me for giving him a son. Quite as if it were all my own unaided doing.

Of course the journey is nothing, especially now we have our own carriage. It is an expedition which Isabella Knightley makes once or twice a year with all her family and usually a new baby in addition. But what more could I say? Mr. Pinkney is, after all, ten years older than me, and although he is genuinely concerned for

7

Edward, I suspect he is also reluctant to leave his books, his club and his home, this pleasant, sunny house to which he has become attached. While he readily concedes that we had a delightful time two years ago when we stayed with you in the school holidays, he reminds me that we were in the process of moving. It was convenient as well as pleasant to be in Highbury.

It is a visit I shall never forget. Everybody was getting married. Harriet Smith to Robert Martin; Emma Woodhouse to Mr. Knightley; Jane Fairfax to Frank Churchill. Then, shortly afterwards, they all began breeding. A baby a year! Heaven help us!

The date, August 1814, is forever engraved on my memory. Lord, how well I recall my *protégée* young Charlotte's look of astonishment and disbelief when I apprised her of the fact that I was with child. She surely thought I was far and away too old, as, heaven knows, so did I. Quite extraordinary that I, who had always disliked children, and who had been married before, was at my advanced age soon to become a mother! The prospect was appalling. Then only three months later Charlotte married Lieutenant Marlowe and soon found herself in the same condition. (I have not heard from her for some time, by the way. I hope nothing is amiss.)

It was during that visit that I first met Mrs. John Knightley. Do you remember? They were staying at Hartfield. She came to call on you and brought her five children—the number she had *then*. You introduced us, and I was able to tell her we shared the same apothecary in London. The connexion through Mr. Wingfield and our subsequent conversations about child-bearing—for at that time I could think and talk of nothing else—established a friendship which I cherish. Mr. Pinkney says she is not my equal in intellect and he wonders what in the world I see in her.

"Well, my love," said I, "we do share one peculiarity."

"Oh," said he, "and pray what may that be?"

"We are both extraordinarily fond of our husbands."

I am sure he thought I was quizzing him. Nevertheless,

dear Mary, however great one's attachment is to one's husband, I believe I could not have survived those months before Edward was born without Isabella. So many women die in childbed; I dreaded the coming ordeal. Well, we have our beautiful boy, and all that is in the past, thank the Lord. I am only trying to convey that a woman friend is quite a boon. But I am telling you what you know already. You have Miss Bates and Mrs. Perry and Mrs. Cole.

Here comes Betty bringing in the darling child with his box of bricks. It is his play time and I have promised to build him a house. You should hear him. Not yet two, and he says, "Make house, pease, mama," so distinctly. His father declares he will grow up a genius.

Your affectionate sister,
Charlotte Pinkney

P.S. No, you did not mention that the Eltons had left. When? Why? What unhappy congregation is encumbered with them now?

Letter 3

(From Mrs. Goddard to Mrs. Pinkney)

The School
Highbury
20 September 1816

My dear Charlotte,

Dinner is over, and I have some time to spare before tea. Writing to you is my cherished recreation, which you might think strange since one of my more laborious tasks as mistress of a school is to compose dispatches to solicitous parents about their daughters' welfare. But those are letters of business. I must weigh my words and consider carefully what I say about their health, their diet, their travel, their education, their music lessons, their pocket money, *and* their flannel petticoats! The list is endless. But to you, dear Charlotte, I can let my thoughts flow uncensored from my pen.

First, I fear I must remonstrate with you over your comments about Emma and Mr. Knightley. It is not at all what a lady should remark, even to her own sister. Most indelicate.

But since you mention the subject, and as you refer yourself to your own apprehensions when you were about to be delivered, perhaps you might spare some compassion for Mr. Woodhouse's feelings on the occasion. I remember at the time Mrs. Perry telling me that he was in mortal dread of Emma's coming *accouchement*. I understand his fears for her safety had constantly to be allayed. So much so, in fact, that it was even half-seriously mooted that she should go to Donwell Abbey for her confinement. But of course her father could not bear to let her out of his sight, and in any event such a suggestion was quite impracticable, the house being shut up for so long with only Mrs. Hodges and William Larkins about the premises. So it was settled that the child would be born at Hartfield.

When the portentous moment came, they were all at some pains (not intended as a pun) to keep Mr. Woodhouse from being aware. Mrs. Weston, by prior arrangement, was sent for. She spent the day with Mr. Woodhouse. He, poor old man, quite unsuspecting, was told that Emma had a headache. I understand that so absorbed was he in talking and playing cards with his beloved "Miss Taylor," as he always insisted on calling Mrs. Weston, that he did not even hear Mr. Perry ride up on his horse.

Hartfield is a well-built house, and evidentally, Mr. Woodhouse heard no footsteps, no bustle, did not know of the advent of his grandson until he was actually in being. He perceived nothing unusual until little Henry Knightley, red-faced and wailing and all wrapped up in shawls, was carried down to the drawing-room and presented to his grandfather. I am sure Mr. Woodhouse must have been flattered that the child was named after him, rather than after his own father. Of course this means that the first cousins, the children of Emma and Isabella, have both the same name, Henry Knightley, but since one is seven years older than the other, and they live in different places, I do not imagine it will signify.

As for your remarks about Jane Fairfax, one must remember in all charity that her health has never been strong, and she has always laboured under a disadvantage. How would you have liked to grow up forever to be remembering your dependent situation and being obliged to be grateful in not one, but *two* households? At Colonel and Mrs. Campbell's, where she was taken in as a child, and at her grandmother and aunt's in Highbury, where she paid occasional visits. Frank Churchill, of course, was in exactly the same position, having been given up by his widowed father at a tender age and adopted by his rich uncle and aunt. I sincerely hope these two young people are now happy together and are making amends to each other for their earlier, most difficult, childhoods. It is their first visit to Highbury since their marriage, so they will be quite a novelty for us all.

An interruption. Two of my girls, twins, Louisa and Lavinia, came romping into my parlour wanting me to admire their quotation books. I was obliged to give them my attention, for they deserve encouragement in a pursuit less frivolous than their usual occupations. I have now sent them off to look up further extracts in the library. You will be amused: I had previously told them they must focus on a subject, and being seventeen, of course one chose Devotion and the other Love.

Since I began this letter, Mrs. Perry has called and informed me that Frank and Jane arrived this afternoon. Her husband happened to be at Randalls when they came—little Anna Weston had some minor indisposition. He thought Jane very pale and delicate-looking. Of course it is not too long since she last lay in. The younger of her two boys is only three months old, the other just over a year. Now I must to my duties. I will continue tomorrow.

21st. Sept: Mrs. Bates's funeral took place this morning. From my window I could see in the distance the procession wending its way to the church. Later Mrs. Cole called and told me what Mr. Cole had to report.

Present were: Frank Churchill (as handsome as ever), Mr. Knightley (looking quite the squire of the neighborhood), Mr. Cole, Mr. Weston, Robert Martin (it was good of him to come all the way from Abbey Mill Farm), Mr. Perry, of course, John Abdy from the Crown (his father was clerk to old Mr. Bates), the Coxes and some of the tradesmen. Mrs. Bates was very well respected, and the older folk remember her when Mr. Bates was vicar and she was in her hey-day.

Miss Bates, I understand, has been quite undone by the death of her mother. I suppose it is natural when you consider how many years of her life she devoted to her. I much regret that I have not myself had an opportunity to see or speak to her. I hope she will be somewhat consoled by the comforts of Randalls and the company of her niece.

Good soul! Heaven knows she deserves some enjoyment. Since her mother has long been too frail to leave home, Miss Bates has had to refuse all invitations to visit Enscombe. Invitations which, according to her, were most pressing, and given not only by Jane and Frank, but also by the old uncle, who continues in excellent health, and who seems to have taken on a new lease of life since Mrs. Churchill's departure from it. Incidentally, the breach with Mr. Weston has been quite reconciled. It was all *her*, the aunt's, doing. In fact Mr. Weston has actually paid a visit to Enscombe, about a year ago, on the occasion of the christening of his first grandson.

The two boys are called Weston and Fairfax. Rather pretentious sort of names. Frank Churchill's notion, perhaps? Presumably it is the modern fashion, and, as Frank does not bear his father's name, it is a fitting compliment to call the first grandson after him, and since Jane is the only surviving child of Lieutenant Fairfax, long since dead, I imagine she wanted to memorialize *her* father, also. Besides, if one lives in a grand place like Enscombe, I infer that William, Thomas or George simply will not do.

The service was taken by Mr. Rutherford. Poor young man, his second funeral in the short time he has been at Highbury. In spite of his rather rumbustious reputation, he performed with due dignity and decorum. He is a gentleman, at least, though very young and green still. But I suppose he will improve with age.

I am sorry. I thought I had told you the Eltons were leaving. Mr. Elton's constant applications to his old college at Oxford finally bore fruit. He was presented to the first vacant living in town. I did not catch the name of the church. To us in Highbury, all London churches with the exception of Westminster Abbey and St. Paul's are one and the same. Whether Mrs. Elton will receive *there* all the consequence which she has ever felt her due, and which was not always supplied by us, the inhabitants of Highbury, who can say?

At least we were spared the long-promised visit of her rich brother and sister, Mr. and Mrs. Suckling of Maple Grove. Much as it was talked of, it never came to pass.

Before they left, Mrs. Elton came to call on me, the first time she has ever done so. One wonders why she should at this juncture decide to pay this civility, unless it was for the pleasure of informing me that one of the *particular* reasons she wished to be in town was so that little Gussie could receive the best possible education! Bless me, the child is not yet two. In general I am disposed to like most people, and of course one would not wish to be *discourteous*, still, I never could take to Mrs. Elton. Nor was I able to forgive Mr. Elton his spitefulness in publicly humiliating little Harriet at the Westons' ball. Well, well, that should be forgotten; one has no business to be dwelling on unpleasant memories. I may say, however, that there is very general relief that they are gone, and the atmosphere in church on Sundays is vastly more Christian than it has been in the past. Ah, not very Christian of *me* to make such remarks.

I daresay, however, that the Eltons will do very well in London where there are more fashionable people. Mrs. Cole tells me that Mr. Cole was up to town on business and actually called on the Eltons. Evidently they were already well-settled in their new parish.

Ever yours aff:ly,
Mary Goddard

P.S. Please try to persuade Mr. Pinkney. It seems to me that you usually gain your wishes in the end. The carriage, so long denied you, is a case in point. Tell him Christmas in Highbury is delightful and much less dirty and *noisy* than London.

Letter 4

(From Charlotte Marlowe to Mrs. Pinkney)

Mrs. Smith's Lodgings
Portsmouth
22 September 1816

My dear Mrs. Pinkney,

I will not dissemble, I will not stoop to conceal the real purpose of this letter by beginning, as is usual, with empty salutations. No, as a sailor's daughter and a sailor's wife, I will face fearlessly forward and come to the point. I am writing to beg a favour of you.

14

Now, surveying those words, I think how uncivil, how abrupt they sound. I am sure you must be saying to yourself, "What right has that ungrateful girl to ask anything of me—she from whom I have not heard for five or six months, at least?"

Dear Mrs. Pinkney, I shall always be grateful to you for all you did for me. If it were not for you, I would never have met my beloved Richard. You are often in my thoughts, you, and Mr. Pinkney and your little Edward. For all I know he might even have a brother or sister by now?

When I married a sailor, I knew life would not be easy. But I was not quite prepared for the hardships we have had to endure, nor did I understand that in peacetime Richard would be gone for so long from home. He is appointed to the Royal Navy anti-slave trade squadron off the west coast of Africa. Of course it is quite wrong that there should still be trafficking in slaves. But I ask myself: Why should it be *our* navy that must stop them? And why should it be *my* husband who is sent so very far away?

He has never seen the baby. Sometimes I feel she may be grown up before Richard ever comes back. That is silly of me, I know, and I am sure it is very ill-bred to verge on complaint, but the children have been sickly, our landlady has been unreasonable, and money has been short. So what with one thing and another we have been in a poor way, and since I could not write cheerfully, I did not write at all.

I do not know what I would have done if my dear father had not been here with me. I think you only met Captain Gordon once when he returned to England after being shipwrecked. You would be amazed, dear Mrs. Pinkney, at how extremely capable he is about the house. I absolutely marvel at what a *man* can turn his hand to. Cooking. Amusing the children. Sewing curtains. Darning. Carpentry. Cleaning our few bits of silver. But when I exclaim in wonder he merely replies, "My dear Charlotte, how do you suppose I and my crew could have survived all those years if we had been useless fellows unable to fend for ourselves?"

I am sure he would like nothing as much as to have a command again. Sometimes he goes down to the platform to view the ships riding at anchor and to reminisce with other old sailors. But my heart aches to see him visibly aging. It is worry. He has no funds and frets that he is a burden on Richard and me.

And that is where I come to the favour I want to ask of you. Good Heavens, I wrote that too hastily. I pray you do not think I am begging. Heaven forbid! I assure you we have enough for our needs, but not a superfluity.

No. Our particular predicament is that my father has received no pension from the navy. Of course he was for so many years to all intents and purposes *dead*, that his records were destroyed. Then when he returned to England and attempted to put his name forward again, he was told to be patient, it was only a matter of time. But nothing happened, and the Admiralty has replied to his inquiries with one excuse after another. He has been writing constantly to London. But with no effect. Now, they do not even condescend to reply. In short, he needs to come up to town to plead with their lordships in person. Your and Mr. Pinkney's kindness when I was at that dreadful seminary of Madame Dubois, emboldens me to hope I may impose upon you once again. I pray it would be not inconvenient to you if my father paid a visit to Hans Place? He expects that a week, or at the most, two, should settle the matter.

I cannot write more. The milk is boiled over and the baby is crying, I must see to her.

Your grateful namesake,
Charlotte Marlowe

P.S. In return for your hospitality my father would be so happy if you had anything that needed attention about the house.

Letter 5

(Mrs. Goddard to Mrs. Pinkney)

The School
Highbury
22 September 1816

I am so outraged, my dear Charlotte, that I must seize my pen and write to you at once to relieve my feelings.

Can you believe that Miss Bates has gone? She has, indeed. Actually left Highbury without a word of farewell and disappeared forever to Yorkshire.

Not, as I understand it, that it was her choice, poor woman. Still, I cannot tell you how distressed I am. She was my closest and oldest friend. I shall miss her as if she had died.

The first intimation of anything untoward came from Mrs. Cole (who has only just left me, by the way). She said that Mr. Cole's coachman was at the Crown seeing about some hay, and was surprised to hear that horses had been ordered to Randalls. She and I were just speculating what this could mean—after all the funeral was only the day before yesterday—when Mrs. Perry called in to say that the Churchills had gone. Yes, gone, and bearing Miss Bates away with them. And on a Sunday, too! It happened that Mr. Perry was again at Randalls visiting little Anna. Apparently Frank Churchill was suddenly in a great hurry about something or other, and insisted on being off. A message was sent to Patty, who was given half an hour to pack up Miss Bates's things. Mr. Weston was left with instructions to deal with the landlord, put the Bateses' furniture in store, and dispose of Patty, herself. Such an arrogant decision! Of course we do not know the whole story. But still, for Frank

Churchill to choose to spend only three nights at Randalls, home of his own father, having taken two days on the road from Yorkshire to reach here, and with the prospect of another two to return, is it rational, my dear Charlotte? Or sensible? It certainly is not considerate. How my heart aches for poor Hetty Bates, grieving for the loss of her mother and now torn away from her home and friends without even a chance to say goodbye.

I wonder how Mr. Weston will justify such behaviour on the part of his son? And what must the good Mrs. Weston be feeling? Of course she will never say, because she is a loyal and faithful woman. But she will certainly have an opinion. Identical to mine, I would wager.

You were right in surmising that Miss Bates would be a great deal less well off than formerly. Mrs. Bates, it seems, lived on an annuity. The expectation, when it was purchased, was that Miss Bates would ultimately marry. In consequence of her mother's death, she is almost penniless. Mr. Cox, the lawyer, intimated to Mr. Perry who told Mrs. Perry who told me, that Miss Bates has only a tiny income from a little capital her father was able to set aside out of his stipend. Not nearly enough to live on.

Well, at Enscombe she will have food and a roof over her head, as well as the daily companionship of her beloved niece. But will she be happy there, living in Yorkshire so far from friends and with so volatile a person as Frank Churchill?

'Tis an odd world, my dear. I feel a little better having confided in you. Frankly, nothing has upset me as much as this for years.

Yours,
Mary

Letter 6

(Mrs. Pinkney to Charlotte Marlowe)

Hans Place
London
23 September 1816

My dear young namesake,

I was mentioning to my sister only two or three days ago that I was concerned—not having heard from you for so long—consequently I was heartily relieved to receive your letter. This will be short, as I have no doubt you would like a reply as expeditiously as possible.

Let me say at once that of course we would be most happy to welcome Captain Gordon at Hans Place. Mr. Pinkney will enjoy conversing with a *man* for a change. We have no male servants, except for the coachman, who lives above the stables in the mews. Mr. Pinkney is quite surrounded by women and children—well, one child, anyway. Edward has no brothers or sisters, thank God, and it would be quite a biblical miracle on a par with Sarah, wife of Abraham, if he had.

We both remember your father well from the joyful occasion of your reunion when he first arrived on these shores and came to meet you at our house. Everything is due to him for all that he suffered. Oh, what wouldn't I give to see some of those fat, sleek wretches at the Admiralty, who never set foot upon a deck, spend a few years on an island off the coast of South America. They would soon find out how they liked it! Pray tell Captain Gordon to come as soon as it suits him, and to stay for as long as he wishes. This from both Mr. Pinkney and myself.

I wish *you* were coming, too. There is a niece of Mr. Pinkney here in town at your old school. She visits us on Sundays for dinner, and I am sure the two of you would enjoy regaling each other with horrid tales of Madame Dubois. It would certainly cheer *her* up to feel someone else had endured the same misery and survived.

My dear young Charlotte, I am sorry to hear you are going through troubling times, and that Lieutenant Marlowe is engaged in such a very distressing business. I hope you are able to hear from him occasionally?

Betty is waiting to take this to the post office. She sends her duty to you.

Your affectionate friend,
Charlotte Pinkney

P.S. There is nothing about the house that needs repair. Please tell your father we are *delighted* to have him. We both hope his quest will be successful.

Letter 7

(From Mrs. Pinkney to Mrs. Goddard)

Hans Place
23 September 1816

I am in your debt for two letters, my dear Mary. I was heartily amused to hear of the birth of Emma's son, and scandalized to learn of the abrupt departure of Miss Bates. It sounds to me all of a piece with what one knows of Frank Churchill's high-handed manners. Power. Ostentation. Only *he* could make such an immediate decision, only *he* could remove with such rapidity from one place to another. I am indeed sorry for you in the loss of your friend. What a prodigious translation for Miss Bates! No doubt her former premises above the shop could be dropped entire into Enscombe breakfast-parlour with room to spare. Mr. Pinkney thinks she will not be happy in such surroundings. But I say, no such thing. What a chance for her. Perhaps she will catch the fancy of the old uncle.

No, you did *not* tell me that the Eltons had moved to town. I wish you had. I could have been on my guard. I want you to know that all London churches are *not* the same. One church has a great cross to bear: the scourge of Mr. and Mrs. Elton. Do you wonder, as you should, which church that might be? I will tell you.

Not being a regular attendant, I did not pay too much attention when it was announced that our incumbent old Dr. Coombs, doddering in the extreme, was retiring, nay, was being forcibly removed by the bishop, and that a new young man was coming in his stead. Last Sunday Mr. Pinkney thought we had been negligent too long, and for the good of our souls we ought to go to church. Imagine my consternation and astonishment, my dear Mary, when whom should I behold roosting in the rectory pew in all her frills and furbelows, but Mrs. Elton, and who should be parading down the aisle with a self-satisfied smirk upon his face and a newly-clean surplice on his back, but Mr. Elton. It was altogether too much for me.

We were not able to avoid them, either. They were standing in the church porch as we left. We were obliged to bow, curtsey, etc. and exchange outwardly civil greetings. Charming weather for this time of year. How did they like their new house? Had I heard from Mrs. Goddard? She, herself, expected a visit from her own sister, shortly. Mrs. Suckling of *Maple Grove* (this latter much emphasized). No doubt I had heard the name. They have not seen each other since her marriage to Mr. Elton. I expressed surprise. No, not at all surprising. Highbury such an awkward place to get at. Nothing to go there for in any event. London so much more interesting.

21

I'll wager it was *she* who contrived this move to town. Though I daresay he was not unwilling. The chagrin of seeing Emma sitting beside Mr. Knightley of a Sunday must have been mortifying. Doubtless Mrs. Elton's large private income did them no disservice in securing this appointment. When I first met her at Bath, as Miss Hawkins, I despised her. But when I encountered her again in Highbury, as Mrs. Elton, I positively disliked her. Little did I think the woman would haunt me wherever I went. Well, I have warned Mr. Pinkney. My soul can go to perdition. He need not expect *me* to attend Divine Service with any great frequency in the future.

Betty has just brought in a note from Isabella Knightley. She says she has been keeping rather quiet since her father's death, and apologises for not having been to call lately. (Personally, I suspect another reason—from a hint dropped by Mr. Wingfield.) They are debating what to do with Hartfield, she tells me. The legacy has forced them into making a decision. With so many children to maintain, Mr. John Knightley cannot contemplate removing from London, at present. Myself, I do not believe he has any inclination to do so. Mr. John Knightley is doing very nicely, I hear, in his profession. The two eldest boys, Henry and John, are already at school, and one of these days will be off to Eton. This takes a certain amount of wherewithal, my dear Mary.

Yours ever,
Charlotte

P.S. Why do you call your new young parson rumbustious? Also, I neglected to mention that I have finally had a letter from Charlotte Marlowe. She is her usual proud, brave self, that we remember, though—reading between the lines— plagued by illness, lack of money and an absent husband. She asks if we will put up her father, Captain Gordon, while he attempts to extract money from the Admiralty that is owed to him.

Letter 8

(From Mrs. Elton to Mrs. Suckling)

St. Stephen's Rectory
Arabella Street
London
23 September 1816

My dear Selina,

Thank goodness that one has been left with a comfortable provision. I should be sorry to have to contrive on *less* than £10,000. To attempt to live upon a clergyman's stipend would be quite intolerable. But as it is, we have been able to have the house new-furnished, and it looks very well. My *caro sposo* and I would not be ashamed *now* of welcoming you and Mr. Suckling and wait only for you to name the day. You must not expect the equal of Maple Grove—but then in town and in a rectory one cannot aspire to the elegance or the extensive grounds of a private estate.

I trust you will not reproach your sister that she has been such a dilatory correspondent. But I have had much to see to—a new housekeeper to get into a regular train, two new men to be instructed in their business. I declare, I have not had a moment to call my own. My instrument, my needle, my paint brush all have been neglected. But now I can report that we are in a fair way to being settled. Very glad, I may tell you, to shake the dust of that miserable Highbury from our feet.

There, even a woman of my resources must eventually feel the lack of elegant society. Once Frank Churchill had married Jane Fairfax and taken her off to Yorkshire, apart from Mrs.

Cole (who lives in a style quite on a par with ourselves, though a little too inclined to invite all and sundry to her house) there was no one worthy of my acquaintance. Knightley was quite removed from society by that puffed-up Emma Woodhouse. How you would stare, my dear Selina, were you to meet her. The intolerable airs she gives herself. You would think she was crowned queen of Highbury. Yet she has never been anywhere, had never even seen the sea until after her wedding when they made a tour to the seaside. But as I was saying, once she had entrapped Knightley she kept him shut up in Hartfield, almost a prisoner, allowing him out only to visit his own property at Donwell Abbey.

Poor fellow! He deserved better. I used to have great hopes of Knightley. He once gave a strawberry party in my honour, you know. I do not understand the hold that woman has over him. Two years has he been dancing attendance on old Mr. Woodhouse.

Still, his emancipation is at hand. I heard from Mrs. Cole that Mr. Woodhouse has finally died. He was a harmless old gentleman, absolutely under the thumb of his daughter, but when I was a bride he was excessively gallant to me, quite an old beau of mine. Now I understand that Queen High and Mighty and her husband and child are preparing to move back to the Abbey.

But enough of Highbury. I would like to forget the place, only I do not seem entirely able. There is always some niggling reminder or other. Imagine, the sister of Mrs. Goddard, mistress of the school there, is actually a member of our congregation! Mrs. Pinkney is several years younger than Mrs. Goddard, and, I may say, several degrees higher in society. Her husband is quite the gentleman. Too good for her in my opinion. I have seen Mrs. Pinkney with Isabella Knightley walking in St. James's Park followed by a troop of nursemaids and small children. Isabella Knightley is sister to the odious Emma. Two sisters married two brothers. There was very little choice in Highbury. They must catch a husband where they can. But why I am recounting these things I do not know since I am trying to cast into oblivion everything to do with that unspeakable place.

How different is London! How much pleasanter it is for my *caro sposo* to preach to an educated audience. Very superior to the inhabitants of Highbury, I assure you. *Here*, the congregation in general comprises a very genteel sort of person with nice refined children. I have high hopes for my little Gussie in the future.

Although it is early days yet, already Philip is appreciated as he deserves, which is more than one could say for Highbury. Oh, I protest! There is that wretched place intruding again.

I will talk of something else. Now the redecoration of the house is finished, we are beginning to entertain. This evening is our first party. I have invited the more superior among the parishioners. Sometime or other I must ask Philip's mother and sisters, but tonight is to be truly elegant with music and ices, fresh flowers and rout cakes. Ah, here is Parker come to worry me about the ices. Really! We have already been into every detail. Servants have brains like sieves, which is why they are servants, I suppose.

Let me know when you can come.

Your affectionate sister,
Augusta Elton

Letter 9

(From Charlotte Marlowe to Mrs. Pinkney)

Mrs. Smith's Lodgings
Portsmouth
24 September 1816

My dear Mrs. Pinkney,

Your kind invitation has cheered this household prodigiously. My father hopes to leave on the coach on Monday for London.

I am sorry to hear your niece is unhappy. *You* rescued me from that terrible place. Cannot you do the same for her?

You ask how I am. I am kept pretty busy about our lodgings, for we have only Becky to help and I am obliged to do a great deal of the cooking myself. I sometimes smile when I think how ignorant I was of domestic arts, and how, that summer before we were married, Mrs. Goddard attempted to warn me what might be in store, and her cook Sarah tried to teach me. How averse I was to either listening or learning! Well, as they say, need's must when the devil drives; I have acquired rather hastily the skills it is necessary for me to possess if we are to survive.

Yes, I do hear from my dearest Richard. But even if I did not, I would not forget him. Every evening I set aside a few quiet moments to gaze at his miniature and imagine I am talking to him. He writes to me every day, even if it is only a few lines, and whenever a fast packet is sailing for England he bundles the letters together and dispatches them. I am always in such a turmoil of excitement when they arrive, I am quite at war with myself. Shall I read them all at once? Or shall I save them to peruse slowly one day at a time, thus eking out the pleasure for as long a period as possible? But of course I never can restrain myself. The temptation is too much. I must gobble them all up at once, and *then* when I know that all is well with him, I read and reread and linger over every word of his dear handwriting, the sight of which brings him so clearly before me.

As it happens I received a packet yesterday. So his news is vivid in my mind. He writes very feelingly about the slave trade, still going on in spite of the Abolition. I do not know how familiar you are with the subject? I, myself, knew nothing until Richard was sent out to Africa. Although the capturing of slaves and the subsequent selling of them in the West Indies or America is now forbidden, slavery itself is still practised in those countries, consequently there is a market, and the slavers continue to be active. Richard writes that it is a system more cruel than one can possibly imagine. Sometimes his descriptions are so graphic I can hardly bear to read them. After the Negroes are captured in the forests of Africa they are packed on board ship on shelves below decks and manacled, sometimes so close together they can only lie on their sides and are unable even to sit upright: this without any proper arrangements for the calls of nature. Of course in such conditions very many of them die. The heat and lack of oxygen below decks in such that candles will not burn. Richard tells me of a woman who gave birth while chained to a corpse. The Negroes are branded like animals with their owner's initials and are taken up on deck once a day and forced to dance and sing for the sake of their health. You can imagine how much the poor things feel like dancing. But, like it or not, they are obliged to do so for a sailor is standing by with a cat-o'-nine-tails, and he relishes the chance to use it. Richard says they can always tell a slaver, even from a distance of several miles, on account of the stink. Whenever they can capture such a vessel and return the Negroes to their own country, he declares it is excessively gratifying.

I hope I have not distressed you by this account, dear

madam, but having so recently read Richard's letters, it is much on my mind.

Here in England we cannot begin to conceive of such things.

Your grateful and affectionate friend,
Charlotte Marlowe

Letter 10

(From Mrs. Goddard to Mrs. Pinkney)

Highbury
Thursday 26 September 1816

Fancy Mr. and Mrs. Elton at your very church! What an extraordinary circumstance. I sympathize, indeed, my dear Charlotte. But at least in a place the size of London you will not be obliged to meet her socially. I regret, however, that you will now be attending Divine Service even *less* frequently than before. What would our dear devout father have said? One's worship should not depend upon the character of the parson. Besides, if you really cannot tolerate Mr. Elton there must be plenty of other churches in London. That, my dear, is a hint for you from your elder sister.

Our new vicar, in many respects is already showing himself an improvement on Mr. Elton. He is a younger son, one of *several* younger sons, of an old established family in the north. Charles Rutherford, I believe, took to the cloth because he had no alternative. He was obliged to earn his living and now the war is over he could not find a place in either the army or the navy. He told the whist club that he misses his Cambridge friends and that he has a passion for hunting, which he used to pursue with his brothers at home, but which is not gratified in Highbury. These remarks were repeated by both Mr. Cole and Mr. Perry to their wives, who, needless to say, passed them on to me. I believe that is how Mr. Rutherford acquired the reputation of being "rumbustious." Apart from this—and one regrets he had no calling to the church—I think he is quite a harmless young man. He is at present rather diffident and shy and not very forthcoming when it comes to talking to the parishioners. But in a few years time, when he is married, I am certain he will settle down and make a most respectable vicar of Highbury. I believe he is also fond of fishing—that does not sound like rumbustious, does it? More contemplative, I should have thought. He has been observed sitting with his rod, all solitary on the river bank, just where it makes a handsome curve enclosing the Abbey Mill Farm. He must be lonely, although I believe he has recently had a friend from his old college visiting him. I've noticed a tall, fair young man in his company walking about the High Street. But that young man has now gone. I believe Mr. Rutherford has been to the Perrys and also to the Coles, but two invitations can hardly be said to constitute a circle of friends or be likely to dispel the desolation I am sure he must feel. Were Mr. and Mrs. Knightley not so engaged with their move just now, I am sure they would have invited him to dine.

Speaking of moving, and thinking of Hartfield, I am convinced Mr. Woodhouse must have been much exercised in his mind before leaving the place to Isabella. Emma was always his favourite daughter. Hartfield is convenient and attractive, but it is not to be compared with Donwell Abbey, being only a notch in the Donwell estate. It would be quite out of the question that Mr. Knightley should continue to live there, even if it had been in his power. He would never renounce Donwell and the tenant farmers, such as Robert Martin, who are dependent upon him.

Both houses have been in the Knightley and Woodhouse families for several generations. Mr. Knightley, although the owner of a very considerable property, is not possessed of more than a moderate income. The fortune which Emma Woodhouse has brought to the marriage, I am sure will in part go to improving the estate. It seems to me quite reasonable that Isabella, the elder daughter, should inherit Hartfield. After all, the John Knightleys have no country place, only the house in Brunswick Square. It is unlikely that Mr. Woodhouse was able to reason all this out, and I would not be at all surprised to learn that he sought Mr. Knightley's advice in the making of his will. I daresay some time or other when the John Knightleys retire they will return to occupy Hartfield, and after them, their son, little Henry Knightley, will inherit. Thus will the worthy Knightley family continue to flourish in Donwell and Highbury. The prospect gives me great satisfaction, even though I shall not be here to see it.

Meantime, as soon as the Abbey can be made ready, the Knightleys are to move. I hear from Sarah that Mrs. Hodges and William Larkins are overjoyed at the prospect. The sometimes dour William has even been heard to whistle lately. He has always been devoted to his master and must have sorely missed him not living on the premises. An hour or two's visit a day to oversee the workings of the estate is no compensation.

Talking of Donwell Abbey reminds me that this morning I was pleasantly surprised when two of my former "daughters" from the Abbey Mill Farm came to call. Robert Martin was in Highbury on business and brought Harriet and his sister Elizabeth along in the pony trap. Mrs. Martin and Elizabeth have a separate cottage on the farm—the younger daughter having married last year. Now I am no matchmaker, but I do wish Elizabeth Martin could meet a suitable man. She is such a very pleasant young woman, and of very sterling character, too. I remember she behaved extremely well when Harriet first refused her brother's offer of marriage. She has had her twenty-first birthday, so it is time she found a husband.

Life at Abbey Mill evidently suits Harriet. She is busily occupied by her poultry, her cows and her young babies. After all the worry she caused me by falling in love with Mr. Elton and every other unsuitable man in Highbury, it is highly gratifying to behold her thus settled. She says she hardly ever sees Mrs.

Knightley. Emma, you remember, was once her greatest friend, and the person whom she most revered. Harriet did not utter this with regret, I am glad to say, I think she is satisfied that it should be so. Probably she cannot forget that Miss Woodhouse once advised her not to marry Robert Martin. Still who knows how it will go in the future? With the Knightleys moving to Donwell, the two families will be living close together, and perhaps there will be more occasion for meetings, though perhaps not.

Emma Knightley is very little seen about Highbury either, though she is as intimate as ever with Mrs. Weston. Now they have, as well as all the previous associations, the mutual additional interest of their children. Little Anna is only fourteen months older than Emma's child. It gives me pause to think that Anna will in two or three years' time be the same age as Emma was when I first came to Highbury and met her and Mrs. Weston (Miss Taylor then), recently arrived at Hartfield to be her governess. Where have the years gone?

Yours aff:ly,
M. Goddard

P.S. I am very sorry to hear that young Charlotte is having a difficult time and that her husband is stationed so far from home. A sailor would not be everybody's choice of husband.

Letter 11

(From Mrs. Pinkney to Mrs. Goddard)

Hans Place
Tues. 1 October 1816

My heart aches, my dear Mary, for your lonely young parson. Poor fellow! A typical cadet of a large family. Our English custom of primogeniture is so unkind to younger sons: there they are, brought up in luxury and ease on the family estate, then when they come of age they are thrown out and obliged to fend for themselves. Naturally this Charles Rutherford, bereft of his home, his brothers, his university friends and his usual occupations, is disconsolate. He has been thrust into a profession for which he is in all probability ill-prepared, has little aptitude and no inclination. Furthermore, he is sent off to a place where he knows nobody, yet is expected to take some kind of lead in village affairs. In my view, the transactions of the Church of England defy comprehension. No pensions for widows, no consideration for their clergy. Of course Mr. Charles Rutherford needs a wife: a cheerful, pleasant, hard-working wife. Out of your vast store of girls, Mary, cannot you provide one? Yes, certainly you can. It just occurs to me. Elizabeth Martin. Promote the match, and you will be performing a double good deed: dispelling the loneliness of one person, and furnishing a husband for the other. Is this not an excellent plan? Mine has been the idea, yours must be the execution.

Everything you have to tell me about Emma and Harriet and the move to Donwell interests me excessively. Mr. Knightley must be a happy man. Having done his duty, he now reaps his reward. *There* is another case of primogeniture—but without hardship: only two brothers, and Mr. John Knightley a successful lawyer. No cause to repine.

Well, Captain Gordon arrived yesterday. Understandably in rather low spirits. He appears quite aged since we saw him last—grey, grizzled, weather-beaten. His manners are a curious mixture of dignity and humility, which in a person of his achievements is pitiable. I surmise that his impoverished state and the fact that he is beholden to relative strangers for hospitality is very distasteful to him. At dinner, Mr. P. had absolutely to press him to accept a glass of wine. He positively refused a second, said he had drunk so little in recent years he was afraid it would go to his head. His clothes are almost threadbare, though very neatly patched, darned and pressed.

He lost no time in going off to the Admiralty early this

morning. He did not volunteer any information on his return, and we did not like to pain him by seeming curious. Over tea this evening, however, he remarked with some bitterness that the country has often treated its best sailors very shabbily. He cited Captain George Vancouver who, on his return from his voyages, was not only subjected to a law suit from one of his crew, but was rewarded for his daring explorations by a pittance on which he could barely subsist.

It must be intolerable to be poor and anxious, when one has formerly been a captain in the Royal Navy in command of a ship with power and authority over a hundred men. Worse, when added to that poverty is the sense of unmerited injustice.

My dear husband is calling to me to blow out the candle and come to bed.

Yours aff:ly,
Charlotte

Letter 12

(From Captain Gordon to Charlotte Marlowe)

Hans Place
London
Wednesday 2 October 1816

My dear Lottie,

A line to let you know I have arrived and am settled here at Hans Place. The coach journey hither was unexpectedly pleasant. I sat next to the coachman and he proved a most agreeable fellow. One of those gentleman drivers one hears about.

Mr. and Mrs. Pinkney make me welcome. She has a tart tongue, but I know it conceals a more tender heart since she was very good to you when you needed a friend. Indeed, one could say she is good to me, taking me in under her roof.

You particularly desired me to tell you about their child. He is very forward for his age, more so, I think, than our little Richard. But that I ascribe to his being the only child of elderly parents. I would judge Mr. Pinkney to be quite as old as I am. He most obviously dotes on the boy. She also, I conclude, though in a less demonstrative manner, at least when I am present. I have an idea that she thinks it shameful to show affection before a stranger.

I went this morning to the Admiralty, but to no purpose. I spoke to the clerk. My name does not appear to be on any list, and I was not successful in gaining an interview with anyone of importance. I have been so long away from public notice that to convince the necessary persons of my eligibility and worthiness, I foresee will be arduous work.

I will not write again unless I have good news. It is only more expense, which can be saved.

Mr. and Mrs. Pinkney send their best wishes.

Ever your aff. father,
A. J. Gordon

P.S. This coming Sunday I am to meet a niece of Mr. Pinkney, a Miss Adams. She is actually a pupil at that same devilish seminary where you were once so miserable.

Letter 13

(From Mrs. Suckling to Mrs. Elton)

Maple Grove
nr. Bristol
2 October 1816

My dear Augusta,

It gives Mr. Suckling and me the greatest satisfaction to think that you and your dear husband are settled in a situation worthy of you. I never liked the thought of your living in a place so retired and with such inferior society as Highbury.

I was also concerned for my niece. When I think what a vulgar coarse person little Gussie would have grown up to be if you had remained in Highbury and been obliged to send her to the school of this woman Mrs. Goddard, you tell me about, I tremble.

I delayed answering yours until I could prevail on Mr. Suckling to settle upon a convenient date for our visit to you. It was unfortunate that we were never able to manage it while you were at Highbury. But from what you say of the place, evidently we missed nothing. Monday, the 25th of November, if it suits you, would suit us. We will leave on Sunday and spend one night on the road. Odious as is the prospect of a night at an inn, at least I shall have with me my own sheets, and it is preferable to travelling in the dark, as we would have to do if we attempted the journey without stopping. Mr. S. says he cannot spare more than a week away. We must be home by the following Sunday. He trusts Mr. Elton is not one of those clerics who objects to Sunday travelling?

I grieve that it is so short a visit. Unfortunately Mr. S. is just now very much occupied by his trade with the West Indies. Since slavery was abolished nine years ago, the whole nature of shipping has changed—that is, if one keeps within the law, which naturally Mr. Suckling would wish to do. He never *himself* actually traded in slaves. In fact you will recall he was always rather a friend to the abolition. So his conscience (which it is now quite the fashion to have, thanks to the Evangelicals) is clear. Still, he often passes the remark that his father had it much easier than he does. When old Mr. Suckling was in charge, it was merely a question of loading up with trinkets and baubles manufactured here, which could be traded with the chiefs in exchange for slaves. Now it is infinitely more intricate and hazardous when salt cod must be collected from Newfoundland and transported to the plantations in the Caribee Islands in trade for sugar and rum. I tell you these things so that you may understand that it is not lack of *inclination* which prevents us coming to you for longer. I am sure you remember how Mr. Suckling and Mr. Bragge used to fly about the country with four horses, driving to London and back twice in one week. I have hopes, therefore, that we can make this expedition a more regular occurrence in the future. There is shopping I wish to do. I particularly desire to visit Wedgwood's showroom, and I hear of a charming little milliner's shop in Paternoster Row, which Mrs. Bragge visited recently. I am determined to have a bonnet as fine as hers. Then there are all the silk merchants at Spitalfield's. I declare, you and I shall have plenty to keep ourselves busy.

Here at Maple Grove, I, myself, am very much occupied. We are making one or two improvements in the grounds. Fine autumn weather is such a good time of year for everything of this sort. That bench round the lime tree in the centre of the lawn which you always admired has been rotting away and in need of replacement. We are also constructing some hot houses so that we can grow our own pine apples, and extending the kitchen garden, building brick walls and so forth. It is not always easy to obtain honest, civil men who will do the necessary work without demanding an extortionate wage, but in these restless times one must put up with what one can get.

Mrs. Smallridge has just been announced. Pray excuse this short letter. The children are being a nuisance and I must send them off to the nursery. If they thought of it, I am sure they would wish to be remembered to their cousin Gussie.

Your affectionate sister,
Selina Suckling

P.S. I note your letter was quite *full* of Highbury. I beg you to put everything to do with that miserable village out of your mind. Do you advise us coming in the chaise or the barouche-landau? We travel with four horses, of course.

Letter 14

(From Mrs. Goddard to Mrs. Pinkney)

Highbury
Wednesday 2 October 1816

Poor Captain Gordon! I do wish him success with all my heart. His having some money of his own would make a considerable difference to the young Marlowes, I conclude.

Well, today, my dear Charlotte, I had the pleasure of meeting Mrs. Weston in Ford's. She is such a delightful woman, and she never varies. I had not had a chance to speak to her by herself since Mrs. Bates died. But this morning there were a number of customers in the shop and neither of us could be served, so we sat on the chairs by the door and had a most comfortable talk.

I am now in possession of the facts concerning the Churchills' sudden departure for Enscombe. The subject came up quite naturally. I simply remarked how much I missed Miss Bates, and that I hoped she was happy in Yorkshire. I was concerned, I said, that she had not written. I did not think she would prove to be such a poor correspondent. Kind-hearted Mrs. Weston looked quite distressed at the mention of Miss Bates not writing, and declared it was most unfortunate they were obliged to leave so hurriedly and that Miss Bates was not able to say goodbye. Apparently an express had come to Randalls from Enscombe. One of the little boys—Weston, I think—had a cold. A nervous nursemaid was concerned.

Mrs. Weston thought at the time that Jane was not unduly anxious. The child had been perfectly well when they left home. But Frank Churchill was bound and determined to leave at once. (I do not really like to imply such a thing, but between you and me, I infer it was almost an *expedient*.) I remarked that Mr. Weston must have been disappointed that the visit of his son should be so abruptly concluded. Mrs. Weston said, yes, he was. But then Mr. Weston was always so good-natured and had such a sanguine temper: since it could not be helped, it must be put up with. One day soon they would all go to Enscombe themselves, and then they could have a long visit together without the affliction of a recent fu7neral, etc. etc. So that, my dear Charlotte, is the story as I was told it. But I continue to puzzle that I have not heard from Hetty Bates. Not one of her old friends in Highbury has had a letter. Is she too distressed to write? Or, is she so busy and happy that she has not time to write? I devoutly hope the latter, though I fear the former.

I did ask Mrs. Weston how Frank and Jane found the little patient when they reached Enscombe. Apparently he was quite recovered. Frank Churchill subsequently wrote to his father in very good spirits that he had invited a party of friends for pheasant shooting, and was pleased to report they got an excellent bag.

In such a household I do wonder how my poor dear Hetty Bates is faring.

Yours with love,
Mary Goddard

Letter 15

(From Mrs. Pinkney to Mrs. Goddard)

Hans Place
Thursday

I am not in the least surprised, my dear Mary, by what you tell me. I suppose Frank Churchill was bored with Highbury—could not endure to stay longer in his father's small house (small, by Enscombe standards) with Miss Bates on top of him talking all day. How fortuitous the arrival of that express from Enscombe! I think so little of Frank Churchill that, if it were possible, I would accuse him of contriving it. In the event, he obviously made the most of the opportunity. Myself, I have had no patience with that young man ever since he failed to deliver the letter you wrote offering young Charlotte a place in your school. It nearly caused a rift between us. Do you remember?

With regard to Miss Bates, one can only hazard a guess as to why you have not heard. Could you not write to her yourself, and inquire how she is?

Well, well. We all have our troubles. You will hardly believe it, but we seem again to be caught up in a web of misery caused in part by that wicked woman Madame Dubois. This time it is Mr. Pinkney's sixteen-year-old niece Sophy who is giving us concern. She has not settled well into Madame's seminary. We knew she would not. From a plantation in Barbadoes to a pretentious school in London is altogether too much of a transition. She ought to have gone to you, at Highbury.

Selfish creature that I am, I'm exceedingly vexed that we have this worry. Her father is so far away, and, having *ignored* our advice, who is it, pray, who has to bear the burden of responsibility for her discontent? Mr. Pinkney and myself, of course. "Not fair," as we used to cry at school. Also, since we no longer live in Sloane Street, next door to the odious Madame, we are not able to be on hand to comfort the child as we could young Charlotte in her time there.

We see Sophy once a week on Sundays. She comes for dinner and eats ravenously. Her table manners leave much to be desired. Evidently the food at the school is as meagre as before. This coming Sunday I look forward to Captain Gordon's being present at table and hope that the conversation will in consequence be elevated above Sophy's continuing complaints about the school and London and how much she hates it.

Here is Mr. Pinkney come to remind me of the time. I must put on my halfboots and prepare to accompany him on our daily walk prescribed by Mr. Wingfield. But I do not repine. I enjoy our conversation and the exercise, which has answered so well with Mr. Pinkney's gout.

Adieu,
Charlotte

Letter 16

(From Mrs. Goddard to Mrs. Pinkney)

Highbury
4 October 1816

My dear *Sister*,

What is a *sister* for if not to lend a sympathetic ear?

Your letter has just come. I am completely taken aback to learn of the existence of a niece of Mr. Pinkney. You have never mentioned her to me before. Why have you not done so? Please pay me the compliment of your confidence. I am quite provoked that you could possibly imagine I would not most *gladly* listen to anything you had to tell me, and help in any way I can.

From what little you say, one cannot help sympathizing. It cannot be easy for the girl to settle into a boarding school, at her age, and in our climate, after the sort of life she doubtless enjoyed in Barbadoes.

A child is like a plant. It has to be transplanted most carefully or it will fail to take root. In my experience eleven or twelve years old, and no more, is the age to be placed in new surroundings. I am thinking of my little Sukey, who came to me when she was six years of age, and who is become quite the joy of my life. So homesick and desolate as she was when she first arrived at school, Highbury is now everything to her. I have had her since the day her father was bereaved, you remember, so she is become almost like my own daughter, even as Harriet Smith once was. Sukey's father, so grief-stricken at the death of her mother, married again last year. His new wife has started her own family and it does not suit her to have Sukey with them. Thus Sukey is left very much here with me, goes home only briefly in the summer holidays. She lives in the regular part of the school, but she creeps into my parlour sometimes for an affectionate little hug and chat. She is such a charming child, I cannot help but love her and do my best to make up for the mother's caresses she has been denied.

You suggest I write to Miss Bates and ask if she is happy. Of course I cannot. If she is *not*, how could she possibly reply? Since it is not in her power to effect any change, it would only be making her more miserable.

Now, Charlotte my dear, I shall be seriously vexed if you do not enlighten me regarding this mysterious niece. What do you mean when you say her father ignored your advice? Pray elucidate.

Yours,
M. Goddard

Letter 17

(From Mrs. Elton to Mrs. Suckling)

St. Stephen's Rectory
Arabella Street
London
4 October 1816

The barouche-landau, I believe, my dear Selina.

If the fine weather continues as it has done, I think it may amuse you to join the morning parade in Hyde Park, and we will cut much more of a figure in the barouche. We might also explore to Kensington Gardens. Alas, Vauxhall is closed at this time of year. But that, I hope, will be an inducement for you to return in the spring. I am promising myself that this will be the first of frequent visits and I fully intend that we shall have a most charming time.

I am planning many select little parties for your entertainment, to which, needless to say, Mr. and Mrs. Pinkney will *not* be invited. Your advice to put Highbury out of my mind is excellent. Philip and I shall have pleasure in introducing you to the more refined and genteel members of the congregation, among whom are many people of influence and quality. A fashionable church such as ours, you understand, draws in a most elegant class of person. These people attract each other, because naturally they wish to be seen by their neighbours on a Sunday. You may be sure I have frequently spoken about you and Mr. Suckling and my brother's importance in shipping in Bristol.

So, you see, my dear Selina, your reputation precedes you. Do bring your finest gowns, therefore. My own dressmaker is making me up several for the winter season. We have had much consultation over the trimming. As you know, I have quite a horror of appearing over-trimmed. Yet it would not do to be too plain. One must dress as befits one's position. Elegance and simplicity are everything, do you not agree?

Oh Lord, here is Parker! I declare, one cannot even write a letter without being interrupted. One has positively no peace from the demands of servants.

In haste and anticipation, I count the days until your arrival.

Augusta Elton

Letter 18

(From Mrs. Pinkney to Mrs. Goddard)

Hans Place
5 October 1816

This is my third letter to you in one week, my dear Mary. Mr. Pinkney asks if it is not a trifle excessive, and complains that I spend too long at my desk when I might be giving him the attention he says he deserves.

"Be still, sir," I cry, "it is of your niece that I write, and you receive more attention than most husbands. Let us hope that my sister will have some useful advice to impart in managing this difficult girl."

He contented himself by replying that he conjectured the post office must soon be declaring a handsome profit from the spate of words pouring from my pen. But I know he is most anxious about Sophy, and would welcome any words of wisdom from one as experienced as yourself. I suggested therefore that the most effectual action he could take under the circumstances was to remove himself and Captain Gordon from the house and to allow me to have the parlour to myself. So he has gone to fetch his greatcoat and change his shoes.

Good Heavens, Mary, how could you so mistake me! It is not from *secrecy* that I have not told you of this girl. I simply felt you had pupils enough of your own to worry over. Sukey may be a joy to you now, but I recall very clearly what you had to endure when she first came to you after her mother died. How unhappy and distracted she was. How you had to keep her always with you. How she slept in your room, and how you never allowed yourself to be out of her sight for one moment. Then even now, today, there are those two or three homesick girls you wrote about. To complain to *you* about a girl at a school, especially a girl of sixteen who should be able to fend for herself, seemed to me on a par with meeting Mr. Wingfield in Regents Street and asking for advice about a trifling cold. Oh, I know I used to write to you about young Charlotte's woes. Never mind. All the more reason for my reluctance to inflict more of the same on you now.

But as you ask, you shall hear. I have sharpened my pen, filled up my ink well, finally seen Mr. Pinkney and Captain Gordon out of the house and watched Betty put Edward down for his nap. All is quiet. If you have leisure to read, I have leisure to write.

Once upon a time Mr. Pinkney's niece was, presumably, an ordinary little English girl living in a Hampshire village. But such have been the circumstances of her life that she has become an extraordinary young woman, wild, unmanageable and completely at odds with everyone at the school. To understand Sophy, one must understand her past. It is a longish tale. Draw up a chair and a footstool, dear Mary, and make yourself comfortable.

I must first explain that I scarcely knew of Sophy's existence myself until a few months ago. Mr. Pinkney had scarcely mentioned his sister, her mother, who died long before we were married. She was many years younger, was still a small child when he was already at Oxford. In the fullness of time she married a Mr. Adams. He, it seems, was a refined person, an Evangelical, rather religious, living in Hampshire in a small way with no money to speak of until he inherited from an uncle a plantation in Barbadoes. (You know me and geography, dear Mary, when Mr. Pinkney told me this I was obliged to take down the atlas to find out where Barbadoes was.) I would hazard a guess that Mr. Adams did the same. For he had never been to the island, and the legacy was entirely unexpected. Now although I am imparting this story in a regular, connected way, the following particulars, which I am about to relate, were acquired, not all at once, as I am telling them to you now, but slowly, over a period of years in voluminous letters from Mr. Adams to Mr. Pinkney.

It seems that at first, and for some time after inheriting the plantation, Mr. Adams had been content to receive the income it produced without inquiring too closely into the manner of its making. Then in 1807, there occurred the Abolishment of the Slave Trade Act, and, as luck would have it, in the same year his overseer fell sick and died. Mr. Adams found he could no longer avoid going out to Barbadoes. So he let his house in Hampshire for a period of two years and set sail from Bristol, taking his wife and daughter with him. Sophy was seven years old.

As you may imagine—and we have all heard of such things here—he was shocked and disgusted by the conditions he found on his plantation. The tales of floggings and cruelties with which he in due course regaled Mr. Pinkney would make your blood run cold. For example, even women big with child were not exempt from being whipped in the field on their bare flesh if their work was unsatisfactory. Then slaves were bartered and sold like horses in the market place, and, like horses, valued by examination of their teeth and physical condition.

Mr. Adams had not been in Barbadoes a year before his wife succumbed of a yellow fever. Naturally he wrote to Mr. Pinkney to apprise him of the death of his sister. Mr. Pinkney, of course, wrote a letter of condolence in return, not expecting to hear anything further, for he had met Mr. Adams only once at their wedding and there had been almost no communication from either his sister or her husband since. But to his surprise, Mr. Adams began to correspond with him regularly. At first Mr.

Pinkney imagined he felt the need to keep in touch with his deceased wife's brother, his child's uncle. Then it transpired that Mr. Pinkney was valued as Mr. Adams's *only* relation (and that not even by blood) and as one of his very few connexions to life in England.

From kindness, Mr. Pinkney felt obliged to reply to Mr. Adams's letters. (Kindness is one of the qualities I most value in Mr. Pinkney, being sometimes deficient in that virtue myself.) So for the past eight years, Mr. Adams has been pouring out his woes and troubles onto Mr. P. Lately, the chief of these has been Sophy's education.

This, as I understand it, was being undertaken by her mother. But when her mother died all attempts at instruction ceased. One cannot imagine anything like masters in a place so out of the way as a Caribee island, and in running the estate her father had as much on his hands as he could do.

Being evidently a very humane person, he began to construct improved accommodation for his slaves, giving them better food and clothes and in general treating them as sentient human beings. This was not particularly well-received by the other plantation owners. But, his consideration operated to his advantage, for his estate was one of the very few spared when the slaves rioted in Barbadoes, which you may have read about happening earlier this year. As he wrote at the time to Mr. Pinkney, taking a leaf from Shakespeare, "Hath not a black man eyes," etc. In fact I believe the motto of the Abolitionists is, "Am I Not a Man and a Brother?"

Ah, here is Betty bringing me a cup of chocolate, with little Edward bustling along behind her. What a little love! You should hear him talk. He cannot say the letter *L*, but he calls out in the sweetest way, "Mama, pease pay wif me." Who could resist him? Certainly not his doting mama.

I must stop, but will continue as soon as I can because I am anxious to hear what you have to say.

C. P.

46

Letter 18 (cont.)

I could not begin again yesterday as soon as I had hoped, my dear Mary. Mr. Pinkney and Captain Gordon returned from their walk before expected. I was obliged to do my duty as wife and hostess. I cannot answer for what Mr. Pinkney would have said if I had started writing again.

If Edward had not woken up early from his nap I might have finished. As it was we rolled his woollen ball about the room until Betty took him off for his bread and milk. He has so many pretty ways—but no. This letter must not be about Edward. I must not get carried away. One day, before he is too old, I hope you will see him. It is of Sophy and her father that I write.

Mr. Adams originally intended his sojourn in Barbadoes to be a temporary affair, hoping that a year or two would see the estate so well-constituted that it could be left with an overseer and he could return home. But nothing was as easy as he anticipated. Before he could carry out such a plan, he had first to learn the business of growing sugar cane. Then one year there was a hurricane, another, a drought, another, sickness decimated the Negroes. For a much longer period than he had ever anticipated, he was, and is, obliged to remain there.

In consequence of these various catastrophes and upheavals such good intentions as he may have had with regard to Sophy's education came to nothing. Of course she ought to have been sent home to England years ago, but Mr. Adams is devotedly fond of the girl and apparently could not bear to part with her. So here she is, now sixteen years of age, abysmally ignorant, has read nothing, cannot spell, has no accomplishments, and no comprehension whatever of the barest social niceties. She is not unpretty. But such looks as she has are spoiled by her uncouth tomboyish ways. She is not at all graceful or refined, lounges about, has no idea how to enter a room or curtsey or even how to sit straight in a chair. I assure you Mr. Pinkney's niece is no ornament to any drawing-room. She is also hampered by the most appalling accent. I am told it is called Creole. Believe me, it is very difficult to understand.

The whole affair is most unfortunate. I believe Mr. Adams to be a thoroughly good man. He has not, as I understand is often the case, taken a Negro woman into his household, and speaks severely of the other planters and their excessive eating, drinking and licentious behaviour.

With regard to Sophy, I can only suppose that he suddenly came to his senses, realized she was now almost grown-up and he could delay her schooling no longer. He wrote to Mr. Pinkney and told him that old friends of the family, a Mr. and Mrs. Blair, also plantation owners and evidently like-minded persons to himself, were taking a passage for home. He was putting Sophy in their charge with instructions that she should be placed in the first seminary in town, no expense to be spared, and would Mr. P. look out for her. The decision was evidently a very hasty one. His letter must have travelled in the same ship as Sophy and the Blairs, because it arrived within a few days of their coming to call to present Sophy to her uncle. Imagine our dismay when this worthy couple informed us that they had already enrolled her in the seminary of Madame Dubois. They, of course, were just the sort of provincial people to be impressed by Madame's airs and graces. That wretched, unprincipled woman had taken advantage of their naiveté and actually gulled them into paying in *July*, as it then was, the fees for an entire year in advance! Of course we expressed our disapprobation. Mr. and Mrs. Blair, who had obviously come expecting praise and approval from Mr. Pinkney for their efficiency and promptitude, were deeply affronted, and shortly thereafter terminated the visit.

As soon as they had departed our doorstep, Mr. Pinkney sat down and wrote to his brother and told him that we had used to live beside the seminary of Madame Dubois and that it was the very last school in England that should have been selected. The Blairs, meantime, had sent a formal note apprising us that they had gone to Scotland for the summer, taking Sophy with them. They did not return to town until September, just in time to deposit her at the school before they themselves sailed for home.

A letter to Barbadoes, depending on the winds, takes a month or more to reach its destination. As you may guess, Mr. Pinkney's remonstrations were in vain. We heard from Mr. Adams only a few days ago. He said that Madame Dubois had been very highly spoken of by his friends, whose judgement he respected (what, pray, could a Barbadoes planter know about London schools?), that the fees had been paid, that it was a fashionable seminary, which was what he desired for his daughter, that Sophy was to learn the harp and Italian, and that he had promised his wife on her deathbed the girl should be properly educated. In short he wished to let the matter stand, and he asked us to support him in his decision. What could we do? The harp, indeed! I never heard such nonsense. We conjecture he believes that if only he spends enough money Sophy will be miraculously transformed into an elegant young woman with the necessary accomplishments to attract an eligible husband. The prospects are not good in Barbadoes, evidently. The men, who are not at all polished, are mostly planters, and would not satisfy Mr. Adams's exalted hopes for his daughter. I can only suppose him to be blinded by his partiality in not realizing the deficiencies of the girl. Since he is always intending to return to England, he wishes to see her settled here. But Sophy, having spent the greater portion of her life in Barbadoes, considers that island home. An example of the uprooted plant you spoke of, my dear Mary. Obviously it is quite useless to tear a sixteen-year-old girl away from a style of living so different from our own and expect her in a single year to acquire refinements of which she has seen and known nothing all her life.

Sophy's case is not in the least like Charlotte Gordon's was three years ago. She has adequate pocket money, and her clothes are quite as elegant as the other pupils, for the worthy couple before they returned to Barbadoes outfitted her handsomely. But, as our old nurse used to say, fine feathers do not make a fine bird. Unhappily, she has not been accepted by her schoolfellows, who tease and despise her for her colonial accent and manners. Her only "friend," if you please, or the only person to whom she can talk, is a young footman, recently employed to assist the butler. He has been at sea, apparently, and once went to Barbadoes in his ship. I think it very unwise, myself, to employ indoor servants in a girls' school. Quite asking for trouble. In the case of Madame it is sheer ostentation, no doubt with the object of impressing people such as Mr. and Mrs. Blair. Sophy told us this man informed her he had got the place of footman because of his fine calves, acquired, one presumes, from climbing the rigging! Sophy is really very young and naive for her age, and seems so wretchedly homesick and unhappy that Mr. Pinkney has written again most forcibly to Mr. Adams.

The other day, trying to draw her out, Mr. Pinkney asked whom at home, apart from her father, she missed most.

"Why my mammy, sir," said she. (One could hardly make out what she said, but I will not puzzle you with trying to reproduce her accent.)

"Your mammy?" said Mr. Pinkney, confused by her odd pronunciation, and thinking she meant his sister, her mother, dead these many years.

"Yes," said the girl, "and what is worse, I can never hear from her."

Mr. Pinkney was even more perplexed. Surely she was not speaking of being unable to receive messages from beyond the grave?

It took some interrogation before it was revealed that the person in question was none other than her old black nurse, who can neither read nor write. She calls her "Mammy" because that is how the woman is known on the plantation. Sophy is obviously devoted to this curious creature. At least I assume she must be curious. Certainly unlike any English nurse such as Isabella or I have for our children. Indeed Sophy has remarked that London is so strange with only *white* people walking about the streets.

"But there are black people here," said Mr. Pinkney.

"Well, I have never seen one," said Sophy in a rude and disbelieving voice.

"You may not yourself have happened to have observed one in the particular area where you are situated," said he most pleasantly, "but that does not mean that they do not exist. I believe, my dear, it is not wise to express so decided an opinion on a subject on which one is not fully informed. For many years now the aristocracy in England have employed black servants."

"Yes, did not Dr. Johnson have one?" said I.

"Indeed," said Mr. Pinkney, "from Jamaica. He was well-known. When Johnson died, Francis Barber was the chief beneficiary of his will."

"There you are, Sophy," I cried, "is that not a pleasant thing to hear? Black servants are not necessarily ill-treated."

"By no means," said Mr. Pinkney. "I understand that no less an artist than Thomas Gainsborough was commissioned to paint a portrait of the Duchess of Montagu's black butler."

"Well, Sophy," said I, "what do you think of that?"

You would suppose she might be abashed or apologetic on learning these things. But not a bit of it. She said nothing, merely muttered and looked sulky. Tell me, what would you do with such a girl? Nothing pleases her. Not even the weather escapes her strictures. Though we have had such a remarkably fine autumn, she constantly complains how cold it is. Of course she feels the change in climate. And after the freedom she enjoyed at home, being immured in a young ladies' seminary must be a form of penal servitude. But then her father should have thought of these things before he kept her so long in such an outlandish place.

There, dear Mary. Now you have the whole of the history

of Sophy Adams. Make of it what you will, and advise us if you can. She comes to dinner again tonight and will be meeting Captain Gordon for the first time.

Adieu,
Charlotte

Letter 19

(From Mrs. Goddard to Mrs. Pinkney)

Highbury
8 October 1816

Poor Sophy! Poor child! It is a terrible change for her, separated from everyone and everything she holds dear. No wonder she is unhappy, and consequently disagreeable. A most pathetic story. I suppose her father was busy all day and this Negro mammy was almost a mother to her in affection, even as Mrs. Weston (Miss Taylor) was to Emma Woodhouse. Or is that too ridiculous a comparison? Perhaps not one Emma would appreciate. I wonder if the woman, herself, came out of a slave ship? Sophy being so much in her company would account for the girl's strange accent and lack of any kind of refinement.

Well, I am glad you have been prevailed upon to divulge these particulars. Your scruples in not doing so before were quite absurd. You might know I would do anything in my power to help, and what I am going to suggest now is that you send Sophy to me at once. I will endeavour to make her happy. In truth she would surely be more at home here in Highbury than at Madame Dubois, even if a country boarding school was not precisely what her father had in mind. I need hardly say that I would be glad to have her without fee, since she is your niece, and since the money for her education has already been spent. I have had to refuse one or two girls since this Michaelmas term began, but somehow or other I will squeeze in another bed, or ask two girls to share, which they are glad enough to do in the winter when it is cold. Among so many, her food will be nothing at all, so I hope this suggestion will solve your difficulty. I must repeat that I think the business to have been very badly managed. As the twig is bent so grows the tree. Her father would have judged better if he had dispatched her years ago, even as Mr. and Mrs. Ludgrove sent their girls to me from India.

Ah yes. I believe I have not elaborated on the Ludgrove twins, possibly because I did not want you to reproach me, dear Charlotte, for acquiring more parlour boarders. It is a subject on which we do not agree and I pray you will make no comment. I am aware that you object to my giving up my privacy and *peace* as you call it. But you see, I *like* girls. I like a cheerful bustle, and I enjoy the company of young people. Besides, I must earn something extra for my retirement. At the moment I am still very vigorous, but a day will come when I will find it too much to be mistress of a school, and shall be glad of a little nest egg. As you may have gathered, Louisa and Lavinia have been with me for some time, but now they have turned seventeen their father has promoted them to be parlour boarders. Mr. Ludgrove is in the East India Company. He and his wife intend coming home early next year.

At all events these two girls are already making my domestic arrangements rather more lively than usual. Louisa and Lavinia are astonishingly alike. I long ago decreed that they should wear, the one, green ribbons, the other, lavender, but mischievous creatures that they are, they delight in teasing, and even five years' acquaintance had not taught me always to distinguish the one from t'other, at least not until they came to live in my part of the house and I saw them across the table at close quarters every day. Louisa is a little more animated than Lavinia, with somewhat of a saucy look, and a different turn to the corners of her mouth. She also has a mole on her neck, but that is not always visible depending on the cut of her gown.

My concern is that since they are no longer in the schoolroom they should have enough to occupy themselves, always a care for me with my parlour boarders. It was for that reason that I originally introduced Harriet Smith at Hartfield. In the twins' case, I insist that they keep on with their music lessons and practise, and that they spend at least a portion of each day in the kitchen with Sarah. There they are supposed to learn some of the rudiments of cookery and the ordering of provisions and the making of menus. Then they have also their samplers to finish. Louisa has got as far as *P*, but Lavinia has only reached *N*. It is not an occupation they relish.

"Whatever will your parents say?" I cry. "Here they have spent their good money sending you to this school for six years, and what have you got to show for it? Shame on you!"

If I do not keep at them they would spend all their time trimming bonnets and gossiping and reading the novels of the likes of Mrs. Radcliffe. Luckily they are fond of exercise, and they do go for prodigious walks about Highbury. They are forever at Ford's for some trifle or other. You might wonder that I allow them so much liberty. But as they are always together, I deem it quite safe. Mr. Knightley sees to it that there are no gypsies lurking about these days. The two girls are happy and good-tempered, so they are a pleasure to have around the house which evidently is not the case with your poor homesick Sophy. Now, I shall expect her as soon as may be.

Yours ever,
M. Goddard

Letter 20

(From Mrs. Pinkney to Mrs. Goddard)

Hans Place
Friday

You are quick to sympathize with Sophy, dear Mary, but I assure you that if you had to put up with her ill-humour, rudeness and complaints, even your patience would be sorely tried. You are excessively generous in volunteering to have her without fee. How will you ever be able to retire if you throw your money about in this manner? I am sure that Mr. Adams from what I hear of him would not dream of thus imposing on you. Besides, he can afford to pay. Unfortunately, Mr. Pinkney, although most touched by your making such a gesture, does not feel he can in all conscience take up your offer. He cannot remove Sophy from the seminary without her father's permission. Although Mr. Adams did not place her absolutely in our charge, if you understand me, it is a moral obligation to look out for her. Mr. Pinkney, however, has written this morning to him with the suggestion. We hope for a favourable reply, though it may be some time in coming.

Well, dear Mary, I am very much amused that I am not the only one not to reveal all. So you have been concealing from me your new parlour boarders! Twins and lively, and of course charming. Your girls always are. I know you enjoy their society and their flirts and gossips. It is just as well that you do. Myself, I prefer boys. But I will say no more on that subject.

Now I am aware that you have Louisa and Lavinia living with you, it occurs to me that lonely Mr. Rutherford might fancy one of them, rather than Elizabeth Martin. But no, on second thoughts, they are only seventeen. They have plenty of time.

One presumes they do not require a husband as urgently as she does.

I must burden you again with the odious topic of Sophy. She came again on Sunday, as usual. We had hoped that conversation would be easier with Captain Gordon present, but at first neither of our guests seemed disposed to speak, until Mr. Pinkney had the happy thought of asking Captain Gordon if he had ever been to Barbadoes.

"Indeed, sir. Several times. A most beautiful island. Not large, but beautiful. A great deal of sugar cane is grown there."

"Ah," said Mr. Pinkney, "my niece lives on a plantation in Barbadoes."

"Indeed?" Turning to Sophy, "You are far from home, Miss Adams."

"Alas, yes, sir," and her eyes filled with tears.

Seeing this, Captain Gordon quickly began to talk of the place and how often he had been there in various ships and how the crew was always pleased when they dropped anchor in Carlisle Bay. The great circle route, he explained, and the prevailing wind meant that Barbadoes was usually the first of the islands they came to, and was the most popular.

This pleased Sophy and she became almost cheerful in describing her home, though the more she talked the more garbled her strange accent became. Unfortunately it was not long before the recalled happiness *there* reminded her of her misery *here*, and soon she was again talking of the school and how much she detested it.

Mr. Pinkney attempted to check her.

"My dear child," said he, "we have all had to put up with unpleasant times in our school days. It is the way of the world."

"Yes," said Captain Gordon, joining in. "I recall very bad days at the Royal Naval Academy. I was only twelve years old and there were occasions when I felt so despairing I thought I would never survive."

"School was loathsome," said Mr. Pinkney. "I remember

being flogged for offences I did not commit. Some, I did, of course." He smiled.

Sophy, however, did not smile back. "No, sir," she said. "They do not flog girls. Only chill them, starve them and make them wretched."

She spoke with such feeling, we were all shocked into silence. Even I was touched, though at the same time I was vexed with her for her lack of breeding in speaking with such vehemence at the dinner table. I cannot tell you, dear Mary, how oddly she talks, saying "suh" instead of sir, and "starff" instead of starve, and "dem" and "dey" instead of them and they.

"My dear Sophy," said Mr. Pinkney. "Surely you exaggerate, surely it cannot be that bad?"

"It is worse than bad. Far worse."

Mr. Pinkney and I exchanged glances. Captain Gordon looked grave.

"Poor young lady," he said. "I am very sorry for you, and sorry, too, that my own dear Charlotte had also to suffer in that dreadful place."

"There is no doubt she did," said I, bracingly, "but now it is all forgotten. One does survive."

Do you think me heartless, Mary? I feel that in a state of affairs regarding which at present there is nothing to be done, too much commiseration is neither helpful nor desirable. Sophy, in spite of her complaints and protestations, has a stubborn quality which repels a more tender solicitude. I suppose one could say she is *angry*, quite possessed of anger at her situation. It is not an attractive attribute, and a most unfortunate one, because really I suppose she is deserving of more compassion than I feel ready to give.

After she had gone (our coachman always fetches and carries her on these occasions) we talked a little about her. Captain Gordon seemed to be much concerned, so I mentioned to him that his own daughter Charlotte's hatred of the school had been quite as great as Sophy's.

57

"Ah, madam," cried he. "Do not distress me!"

"That was not my intention, sir. I merely wished to point out that young people often have great powers of resistance."

"When I was marooned on that island," said he, seemingly determined to justify himself, which, heaven knows, was not necessary, "I had no notion what had become of my family, I was not even aware that my dear wife had died, or that my wife's aunt had undertaken Charlotte's maintenance, let alone sent her to that frightful place."

"How could you know, my dear sir," said I. "Do not reproach yourself, I pray."

"Dear, madam," said he, "your kindness to my daughter in extricating her from an impossible situation will never be forgotten by either herself or me."

"Well, well," said Mr. Pinkney, "it all came right in the end. Your daughter is now happily married to Lieutenant Marlowe."

"True," said Captain Gordon, "if only . . ." He stopped. I am sure he was going to say, if only they had more money. As it was he merely said good night, picked up his candle and went to bed.

Of course I feel sorry for Sophy. But as you have gathered I simply cannot warm to the girl as I did to Charlotte. Charlotte had her pride, but she was also anxious to please and was grateful for anything one did for her. This Sophy does not care a fig what we or anybody else thinks. She is a completely different sort of young woman, not nearly so likeable as Charlotte. Still, she is Mr. Pinkney's own niece, and he feels a responsibility towards her, especially as we are her only relations, and her father is so far away.

Adieu,
Charlotte

Letter 21

Highbury
14 October 1816

I am sorry, my dear Charlotte, that you do not feel you can send Sophy to me. That means, I suppose, that you must continue to put up with her. She does sound an odd girl, and difficult to manage. Under the circumstances I wonder how much I could have done to improve her temper. One thing I am sure of. She would have been less miserable at Highbury. There would be enough to eat, for one thing. And for another, no one would be unkind to her. *That*, I would *not* allow. Well, let us hope that the winds are fair, the ships speedy and a reply to Mr. Pinkney's second letter comes soon.

Great news! Today the Knightleys moved back to Donwell. I do not need to tell you, my dear Charlotte, that in the annals of Highbury this is a notable event.

The place was certainly more than ready to receive them. When the move was in contemplation, Mrs. Hodges eagerly employed a positive army of disengaged people to scrub and clean. One of them was the Bateses' Patty, who gave my maid Alice all the particulars. (Alice came back this term, by the way, her child Mary is being kept by her friend until she is old enough to be with her here.) But I digress. Patty said the Abbey was positively shining. There has been much beatings of carpets, brushing of furniture, washing of windows and china and polishing of silver going on for at least a fortnight. Mrs. Hodges waxed quite sentimental, evidently, and declared she had never seen the Abbey show such a bright and happy face as it now did to welcome home the return of the master. The move seemed quite in the form of a royal procession. Both Mr. Cole and Mr. Weston lent their carriages, these were in addition to those from Hartfield and Donwell. Then there was the butcher's cart, and William Larkins with a waggon, and Robert Martin came over with two of his labourers and a couple of drays from the Abbey Mill Farm. The Hartfield servants have gone with them—so there was a large number of people to be accommodated and transported together with their clothes and possessions as well as various items of furniture—though I understand that much of it has been left behind, including the family portraits, for the John Knightleys. *He*, by the way, was supposed to come down from town to supervise and give moral support. But at the last moment business prevented him.

I am told that Emma was quite affected at leaving her old home. Mrs. Weston was spending the day with her, and I am sure was a great comfort. One remembers Mrs. Elton saying, or being reported as saying, that it was "quite one of the evils of matrimony" that a woman should give up her own home to settle in her husband's. But since Donwell is a house Emma has known all her life, one need not, I think, feel too much sympathy. Besides, she will have Serle and everyone she is used to about her. Luckily Serle and Mrs. Hodges have always esteemed each other, so no friction is to be anticipated there. It is not, therefore, for Emma, the adjustment most brides have to make upon marriage. Well, my dear Charlotte, you know all about that. Such was the case in both your marriages. First to Yorkshire, then to London. As for the Knightleys, although they have only one child at present, I hope they will have more, and fill up some of the empty rooms. Donwell Abbey, so large and rambling, positively calls out for a large family party. But so far Emma has not proved so abundant as her sister.

My young ladies had great pleasure in watching all the goings-on. Miss Prince and Miss Richardson took some of the girls for their walk in that direction. I think the teachers enjoyed the circumstance quite as much as their pupils. Louisa and

Lavinia, being parlour boarders, could do as they pleased, and found great entertainment in watching from the elevation of a stile halfway along the Donwell Road. It was one of them, who from this vantage point, told me she saw a tear rolling down Emma's cheek. Poor Emma.

There is a rumour that Hartfield is to be let.

Your aff. sister,
M. Goddard

Letter 22

(Mrs. Pinkney to Mrs. Goddard)

Hans Place
18 October 1816

Do not feel obliged, my dear Mary, when you write to me to talk of Sophy. I am quite weary of the topic, and very glad to hear about the grand move to Donwell Abbey. Imagine the proud Emma shedding a tear! I am not very kindly disposed towards Emma, because she refused, no, not refused, that is too strong a word, because she made no attempt to meet me when we stayed with you in Highbury. She is not friendly and unpretending like her sister, but proud and snobbish. I will only give her credit, because *you* do, for looking after her tiresome old father. I concede she must have some other merit I am unaware of, since she has gained the love of such a superior gentleman as you have always claimed Mr. Knightley to be. Of course Mr. John Knightley ought to have been present on the occasion of the move to Donwell, especially as he is now the owner of Hartfield, but with *him* you can be assured that business always takes precedence over friendship. I believe it was something at the Admiralty which kept him away.

I heard this from Isabella herself. She came to call today and intimated that there will be a change at Highbury that will affect you all. I asked her to explain, but she said she had given her word to her husband that she would say nothing until all was signed and settled. I conjecture, as you say, that they intend to let Hartfield. Knowing Mr. John Knightley, it is entirely understandable that he should not wish the house to stand empty and that he wants to realize some return on his property as soon as possible.

Isabella is such a sweet woman. I quite marvel at her sweetness, so unlike is she to me. I never see as much of her as I would wish, and lately I have not seen her at all. When she called, neither Mr. Pinkney nor Captain Gordon was at home, so we had a comfortable coze. I was right in suspecting that it was not just mourning for Mr. Woodhouse that kept her away. She confessed that indeed she is breeding again. Her eighth! I remember Mr. Wingfield remarking before I met her, and I have since observed it for myself, that an addition to her nursery is more or less an annual affair. I think it extremely selfish of Mr. John Knightley. If I were she I should insist upon separate bedrooms.

He may be very clever at his work. And no doubt he is a devoted father, but I avoid him if I can. He does not converse easily. I do not understand Isabella's attachment. I suppose this decision to let has been made because with so large a family—and heaven only knows how many more children Isabella is likely to produce in the future—there is no hope of their moving to Highbury for many years.

While we were together little Edward ran into the room and came to me to be lifted up and put upon my lap and kissed and caressed. Poor Isabella looked on quite wistfully, and remarked that she remembered when Henry was her only child, and that it was such a pleasure having only one because you could love and cherish it as much as you chose. With the number she has now, she said, there is not leisure to bestow affection or attention on any single one to any degree. As soon as she had made this involuntary remark, she retracted it. Said, of course she would not do without any of her dear children for all the world. Poor Isabella! In spite of her supposedly adequate number of nursery maids she often looks absolutely worn out.

Ever yours,
Charlotte

Letter 23

(From Mrs. Goddard to Mrs. Pinkney)

Highbury
25 October 1816

Now I really must give you a gentle scolding, my dear Charlotte. Because *you* would not like a large family, and do not care for children except your own beloved little Edward, I do not think you should censure Mr. and Mrs. John Knightley. Many people *like* to have a lot of children about them, and are proud to be the parents of handsome, tall sons and pretty, charming daughters. Look at our own gracious King George and Queen Charlotte and their family. Fifteen, is it not?

Mrs. John Knightley, ever since she married, has been a woman who lives for her husband and children. Whenever she comes to Highbury and calls to show me her latest baby, it is with the greatest pride. She may be a little tired now, when her children are all so young, but the time will surely come when they will be a source of satisfaction and enjoyment. Dear Charlotte, forgive this little lecture, but I felt I must draw your attention to another point of view.

Now for my main news, which you must have been expecting, and of which you gave me a hint in your last. Hartfield is indeed let! My authority is no less a person than Mr. Knightley, himself. He told me after church on Sunday. Imagine, new people coming to Highbury! The Woodhouses having lived at Hartfield for so long, it is extraordinary to think that the house is now to be occupied by strangers.

Such excitement in our little town. The circumstance almost rivals the occasion when Harriet was threatened by the gypsies.

Mrs. Cole called today and gave me all the particulars which Mr. Knightley did not divulge. Through Mr. Cole, she seems to be very well versed in the matter. That gentlemen's whist club is a positive mine of information. Who pretends that men do not gossip? She says the let was arranged by word of mouth. The tenant is the tall fair young man who was staying recently with Mr. Rutherford at the Vicarage. His name is Pringle. He is from Liverpool and he wishes to remove to the south of England. His forbears have been merchants in a good way in trade, rising in respectability, as well as in wealth, for some time. The father has recently died, apparently, leaving this William Pringle, the only son, a large fortune. The young man was at Cambridge with our vicar, and wishes to settle near him. It was his, Mr. Rutherford's suggestion. He, knowing that Hartfield would be vacant, set the wheels in motion. Whether he mentioned it to Mr. Knightley first, Mrs. Cole was uncertain, but somehow or other Mr. John Knightley was approached, and the matter settled forthwith.

As you surmise, the John Knightleys have no intention of occupying Hartfield until he retires. If they should come down at Christmas and at Easter, which has been their usual practice, they will stay at Donwell. This is what they used to do every other year in any event, alternate years being given to Hartfield. As for this young man, his mother is to live with him and keep his house. We also hear he is planning to keep a pack of hounds. Such goings on! Can you imagine a "View Halloo," a hunting horn and several dozen horsemen careering through our quiet village High Street.

The perturbation among the girls at this school is something to behold. An eligible young man at Hartfield! *Two* eligible young men, if you count Mr. Rutherford. Louisa and Lavinia talk of nothing else. I am sure I do not know where they think they will see, let alone meet, these young gentlemen. Apart from church, I think it must remain admiration from afar.

Aff:ly,
M. Goddard

Letter 24

(Mrs. Pinkney to Mrs. Goddard)

Hans Place
28 October 1816

You never can forget that you are my older sister, can you, my dear Mary? But I take into account your years as mistress of a school and accept your rebuke. In future Isabella may have as many children as she likes—or, as Mr. John Knightley likes—and I will say never another word.

I am delighted for your sake that Hartfield should be occupied: to have it standing empty would not add to the social life of Highbury. But tenants from Liverpool! It does not sound very promising. And is it not strange that from such a background the young man should like hunting?

I have nothing particularly joyous to report here. Captain Gordon has been with us for four weeks now, looking more careworn every day. I do not know what we can do to help him. I discuss it with Mr. Pinkney from time to time, but since his friends were always scholars, he has never had any acquaintance in the navy, and knows no one to approach in the matter. We have felt obliged to stay at home in the evenings to keep Captain Gordon company, and have consequently declined sev-

eral invitations. Most tedious. Mr. Pinkney, ever kind and solicitous, fears he might become too despondent if we were to
leave him alone. So we divert him, either by Mr. Pinkney offering a game of chess, or billiards, or the three of us playing
loo together, for *very* low stakes. If either Mr. P. or I seems likely
to be in danger of winning, we make some foolish play or other
so we do not. I hope Captain Gordon does not suspect us, because I believe these innocent amusements do take his mind off
his troubles. He seems to enjoy cards, which makes the sacrifice on our part quite worthwhile. I know Mr. P. would much
prefer to read. Captain Gordon told us that on the desert island
they so wished for chess that they actually attempted to manu-
facture the pieces out of stones and twigs. The board, they drew
on the sand. The result was crude, but they were able to play
after a fashion.

Adieu,
Charlotte

Letter 25

(From Mrs. Goddard to Mrs. Pinkney)

Highbury
29 October 1816

Our new neighbours have arrived. I must write, my dear
Charlotte, to report on the event.

These people let no grass grow under their feet. Mrs.
Pringle and her son (or should it be, Mr. Pringle and his
mother?) moved into Hartfield today. A great train of waggons
came down from London and trundled through the High Street

with a quantity of servants, more, I should have thought, than were necessary for two people. Bringing up the rear was a grand carriage—though without a crest.

I do not know what difference the Pringles will make to our life in Highbury, but their presence is bound to have some effect. If they are as affluent as all evidence points to their being, I imagine they will keep themselves to themselves and not mix with the rest of us humbler folk. Well, we shall see. Poor Emma Knightley must be having some qualms. Mrs. Perry saw her passing in her carriage on her way to Randalls just as the bustle was at its most feverish.

I am happy to report that at last we have heard from Miss Bates. She must have sat down to a great day of letter-writing, for Mrs. Perry, Mrs. Cole and myself were all recipients. She appears to have said much the same to each of us. She apologises for leaving without saying farewell. Unfortunately it was unavoidable. (Of course, we now know how *that* was.) She declares, as one might expect, that everyone at Enscombe is most kind. It is a handsome place, and never was a woman so fortunate, etc. etc. She admits to missing Highbury, but the children are very sweet and she expects she will soon get used to Yorkshire, which has very fine and striking views. She does not elaborate on any of the personal details one would like to know, such as what she is actually feeling, how she fills her time, and whether she has adjusted to such a radical change of living.

Alas! In this lack of candour, so foreign to her nature, I suspect unhappiness. I fear fine and striking views are poor consolation for old friends.

She remarks that Frank Churchill, in spite of her protestations to the contrary, felt concerned that the children would disturb her, and positively insisted that she be given a bedroom and sitting-room in the east wing at some distance from the rest of the party. You can draw your own conclusions. Of course one knows quite well that she would like nothing better than to be in the very heart and centre of family affairs.

Oh dear, I do so often think of her, and constantly miss her cheerful ways and good-humoured chat. Highbury, not Enscombe, is where she belongs. The tradespeople in the village always inquire after her—Mrs. Stokes of the Crown, Mrs. Ford of the shop—"Have you heard from Miss Bates, m'am, how does she do?" Poor soul! One can only assume that she has nothing to occupy herself, and sits all alone and friendless in her east wing room.

Yours affect:ly,
Mary Goddard

Letter 26

(From Mrs. Pinkney to Mrs. Goddard)

Hans Place
31 October 1816

Ha! my dear Mary. It is just as I thought. Frank Churchill wants Miss Bates as far removed as possible from his sight. It is not to be wondered at that a smart and fashionable young man finds her too much to put up with. A thousand pities they did not buy her a small annuity, and leave her in peace at Highbury. Surely they can well afford it? No, I suppose it is difficult. Jane has no money of her own, has she? She is not exactly in a position to suggest to her husband, or for that matter to the old uncle, who, I suppose, still holds the purse strings, that they should pension off her aunt. Well, well, if Miss Bates is not happy in the east wing, I suggest her only recourse is to set her cap at the uncle. Nothing else to be done.

So your new neighbours have moved in. I wish you joy of them. Whether they will be a source of pleasure or of aggravation remains to be seen. Certainly they must make a *difference* to you all. A young man, newly arrived in a place, single and with money, is bound to create some kind of stir and change. I shall hope to hear of interesting developments in Highbury.

This note is hardly worth your paying for. But I am preoccupied with trying to do something for Captain Gordon. Sophy, too, continues to plague us. Why does one feel responsible for other people? I suppose it is being brought up in a parsonage. So tiresome!

Yours aff:ly,
Charlotte

Letter 27

(From Mrs. Goddard to Mrs. Pinkney)

Highbury
1 November 1816

Charlotte, I beg you will not be facetious at the expense of my old friend. Marry Mr. Churchill, indeed! What can you be thinking of? I have no patience with this kind of smart remark. It is hurtful and unfeeling. And why should it be tiresome to do something for others less fortunate than oneself? These sentiments are not worthy of you.

Yours,
M. Goddard

Letter 28

(From Mrs. Pinkney to Mrs. Goddard)

Hans Place
4 November 1816

I am not surprised you wrote as you did. I am very sorry, my dear Mary. I know how concerned you are for the welfare of Miss Bates. It was wrong of me not to consider your sensibilities. You know how quick is my tongue. I cannot resist sometimes the temptation to a *riposte*. But I hope my heart is in the right place, even though my tongue is not under such good government as it ought to be. I feel nothing but goodwill towards Miss Bates, and sincerely hope she may prosper. Forgive me, as you have often done before.

Confident that you will do so, and trusting to your benevolence, I shall write as if nothing had happened and assume that all is well between us, which I fervently hope to be the case.

Yesterday, Sunday, Sophy was round again as usual. As soon as she walked in the door she immediately held out her hands and desired me to inspect them. The tips of her fingers were all raw and bleeding.

"That," said she, "is from playing the harp. The master sits in the room and forces his pupils to practise for one hour before him."

I expressed sympathy and offered her some lotion, but really, dear Mary, I was quite shocked. I suppose that is how the pupils at that seminary acquire a reputation as great practioners of music! It really is a most wretched place.

In spite of her *fingers*, however, I am pleased to report that her *face* has lately worn a slightly more agreeable, or should I say determined, expression, which makes us hope that she is re-

70

solved to see this school year through and make the best of it. Today she heard from her father promising to come out at the end of July and either take her back to Barbadoes, or, himself to settle in England. Unfortunately there was no mention of Mr. Pinkney's letter.

As we sat at the table, Captain Gordon, Mr. Pinkney and I, we pointed out to her that from now to July is only eight months, and that is thirty-two Sundays (when she comes to dine with us). Mr. Pinkney suggested she make a calendar and tick the Sundays off.

"I used to do that sort of thing when I was young," said he. "It makes the time pass more quickly. There is a certain satisfaction in striking off the days. You can keep the calendar here, if you wish. Then whenever you come, you can mark it and see your progress."

"Thirty-two Sundays is a long time, sir," she said. "There are seven days between each Sunday."

"Come now," said Mr. Pinkney. "I would call it six."

She looked obstinate, but did not contradict him, only muttered under her breath which I heard and he did not that every hour was an eternity, or an age or something of that sort. She then said that one person at least understood what it was like to be so far from home, and she began to tell us with some animation of the footman with whom she speaks about Barbadoes.

"Where does he come from?" asked Mr. Pinkney.

"From Ireland, sir."

"What sort of person is this young man?"

"Oh, a very fine young man," said she, artlessly. "He is six foot tall and very handsome. I overheard Madame Dubois ask the housekeeper how he was getting on, for he only started last month. The housekeeper said, 'Madame, he must have kissed the Blarney Stone, that one. He could charm the birds from the trees, and they'd gladly fetch him anything he wished for.' "

Dear Mary, you can imagine how alarmed I was at this representation.

"How is it," I asked, "that you are able to converse with this

71

person? It is rather a *faux pas*, my dear, rather *unusual* to make a practice of consorting with a servant."

"It is not so in Barbadoes," said she. "I often talk to the slaves who work in the house."

"But this is England," said I. "Pray, however do you contrive such meetings?"

"Oh, in the butler's pantry. In the evening, after tea. There is nobody about then. Sometimes he polishes a bit of silver, just in case, you know, anyone should come in. But at that time the other servants are all in the servants' hall."

Worse and worse. Only it was spoken so guilelessly, so naively, as if it were the most normal thing in the world for a young lady in a seminary to be haunting the butler's pantry after hours and hobnobbing with a footman.

"Does Madame Dubois not object?"

"She does not know, madam. She is not in at that time."

Mr. Pinkney and I exchanged glances. We both remembered how the depraved woman would go out gallivanting of an evening pursuing her own social life, leaving the teachers in charge, who, for their part, were quite indifferent as to the welfare of the pupils in their care.

"Do you know his name, child?" asked Mr. Pinkney.

"Oh, yes, of course. His name is Paddy O'Ryan, though Madame Dubois and the butler always call him Robert. I do not know why that should be."

"Because footmen are always called 'Robert' even as coachmen are always called 'James'," said I.

"How very strange," she replied. "I never heard of such a thing."

"My dear," said I, "I am sure that is why your father has sent you to England. No doubt there are many such customs you have not heard of. If one is to live in society, it is the sort of information one should possess."

"But I do not wish to live in society," said she. "And of what use is it to know anything so stupid?"

"Of what use, indeed?" laughed Mr. Pinkney. "I am sure

it would not help one to survive on a desert island off the coast of South America, eh, Gordon?"

But Captain Gordon did not smile. "I suppose, my dear Miss Adams, that here in London you sometimes feel as if *you* were cast up on a foreign shore."

"Indeed I do," said Sophy feelingly.

"The same as I and my crew did when we were shipwrecked. We used to sit for hours and talk of home. It is a great comfort to speak to a sympathetic person familiar with a place which is dear to one."

"Oh yes, to be sure." Sophy's face brightened. "That is exactly so. Paddy and me talk a vast deal about Barbadoes. It is a very small island, as you know, sir, and Paddy knows it well. He even recollects my favourite cove where the sand is so white and the sea so blue, and he remembers one particular palm tree and the way it hangs out over the water. He says he would like to live there one day, if ever he had the chance. He does not intend to spend his life being a footman."

There was a moment's silence after this strange effusion. Mr. Pinkney and I were temporarily speechless.

"And what would he propose to do, pray?" said I, recovering myself.

"Oh, I don't know," said she, "but Paddy can turn his hand to almost anything."

"He would be a good person to be with on a desert island, then," said Captain Gordon, kindly.

"Well, my dear," said Mr. Pinkney, "let us hope that help is on its way. I have written again to your father and represented your case to him once more. If he gives leave, we will send you to Mrs. Pinkney's sister's school at Highbury."

"Yes, Sophy," said I, "and *there* you need not trouble your head about what to call a footman. The question will not arise. Mrs. Goddard is not that sort of woman, nor is her establishment that kind of school."

"It may be better than at Madame Dubois," said she ungraciously. "Only I can like no school as well as home. Besides,

73

I would miss Paddy if you sent me there. Anyway, it will be weeks and weeks before you can receive a reply."

"Undoubtedly it will, my dear Sophy," said Mr. Pinkney.

The subject was discussed no more, and soon afterwards it was time for her to leave.

When Mr. Pinkney and I were safely in the privacy of our own bedroom I asked him if he was not concerned that his niece should be on such intimate terms with this sailor turned footman.

"I hope she may not get into any kind of scrape," said I. "It is a very unsuitable liaison. Do you not think we ought to inform Madame Dubois?"

"My dear," said he, "do not fret yourself. I would hardly call it a liaison. More a harmless friendship. She is homesick and he talks to her of home. I think she would not speak so openly about him if there was any . . ." He paused, Mr. Pinkney is very correct, even to me, his wife who shares his bed—I could almost fancy him blushing. He hurried on. "If there was any impropriety, anything to conceal, I think she would not talk so openly as she does."

And thus the matter ended.

Adieu,
Charlotte

Letter 29

(From Mrs. Goddard to Mrs. Pinkney)

Highbury
5 November 1816

Thank you for your apology, my dear Charlotte. I was unnecessarily sharp. The offence did not warrant it. It was only that I was so concerned for my old friend, and you seemed to be making light of her troubles. My excuse is that I had a most tormenting headache after an excessively vexing morning. The kitchen chimney caught fire and every single person in the school had to remove from the premises. The girls, I might say, enjoyed themselves hugely standing about outside, gossiping and watching, with many fervent hopes, ill-concealed, that the whole place would burn down and they would be relieved of the burden of doing their lessons. Very entertaining for them, very distressing for me. Eventually John and the garden boy climbed up on the roof and with several buckets of water handed up to them succeeded in extinguishing the flames. The resulting liquid sooty mess in the kitchen, and Sarah's fury at the extra work she and the maids were put to to clean it up, does not bear thinking about. The consequence of this debacle is that I am afraid you bore the brunt of my ill humour. It is therefore my turn to be sorry.

Well, if it is not one thing, it is another. Miss Nash is ill. Nothing serious, a bad cold. She is subject to colds, and Mr. Perry has prescribed two or three days in bed, I have been upstairs giving her hot lemon and honey to drink and a mustard plaster for her chest. She looks very comfortable. I would not mind a day in bed, myself! As it is I have had to teach her classes in French and Greek Mythology as well as see to everything else about the school.

I did feel, however, that it was important for me to write at once and express my opinion after receiving your letter this morning. From what you say about your niece and the footman, it seems to *me* there *is* some cause for concern. I think Mr. Pinkney is mistaken. He has lived retired from the world. Marrying late in life, and for many years shut up with other learned men at Oxford, what can he know of the mind and heart of a young girl? Let us hope, indeed, that it is a perfectly harmless friendship, and pray that this charming Irishman does not take advantage of her. The sooner you can get her away from him and to me, the better, though it does not sound as if Sophy would be willing to come or be content at any school, and of course your hands are tied, until you hear from her father.

Guy Fawkes day today. How time flies! I declare it will soon be Christmas. The little girls have been chanting,

Remember, remember the Fifth of November
Gunpowder, treason and plot.

Do you recollect how much we used to enjoy that day? Tonight there will be a bonfire on the common field. I have given John and Sarah and most of the servants the evening off. Heaven knows, they deserve it. Needless to say, the older girls also begged to be allowed to go under the supervision of a teacher. I felt very unkind (and unpopular) but they will remain here, safe in their beds. I made the excuse of Miss Nash's indisposition. But really, Guy Fawkes can be such a rowdy occasion, and there's no telling what those Morris dancers will not get up to after they have been imbibing. I have the parents and their trust in me to consider.

Yours aff:ly,
M. Goddard

Letter 30

(From Mrs. Pinkney to Mrs. Goddard)

Hans Place
6 November 1816

This is only a note, my dear Mary, to thank you for your apology.

How alarming! A chimney fire. I am thankful to say that I have never experienced such a thing. No wonder you were cross. I confess I was a little surprised because you are always so even-tempered.

I have conveyed your opinion to Mr. Pinkney. He is still not wholly convinced. Dear man, he likes to think always the best of everyone—which is what I love about him, perhaps because I, myself, think always the worst. Well, at least I am never disappointed.

Now he is waiting for me to take our walk.

Adieu,

C.

Letter 31

(From Mrs. Goddard to Mrs. Pinkney)

Highbury

8 November 1816

I have such an extraordinary circumstance to relate, my dear Charlotte, that I cannot resist sitting down, in this my first leisure moment, to tell you about it, even though it is after eleven o'clock, and I have no business to be thus burning the midnight oil.

I have just seen Louisa and Lavinia off to bed. We have had an amazingly busy evening.

Here is what happened. This morning I was sitting at my desk doing my accounts—luckily, Miss Nash is up and about again—when Alice knocked on the parlour door and announced a strange lady was here to see me.

"A strange lady! Whoever can it be?"

"I have never seen her before, m'am," said Alice, as she handed me a card.

77

I glanced at the name and hastily put my papers away in my blotter. "By all means show her up."

In a moment or two, in walked a nice-looking, unpretentious sort of woman, simply dressed, with a round, good-natured face, brown hair and a brown gown. Have you guessed who it was? Mrs. Pringle, new tenant of Hartfield.

"How do you do, Mrs. Goddard," said she.

"How do you do, Mrs. Pringle," said I.

"Do forgive me, m'am, for calling on you like this without an introduction."

"Not at all," said I, indicating my armchair by the fire. "Pray sit down. I was intending to call on you, myself, but I thought I should wait until you had time to settle."

"Oh, we northerners are very quick when we want to be," said she smiling, as she seated herself. "Besides Hartfield is pretty well furnished. It did not take the servants long to hang our few pictures and arrange our things." She paused and looked about the room. "This is a very cosy parlour."

"I am glad you think so, m'am."

"The fancy work is charming."

"Most of it was done by my pupils."

"I have been anxious to make your acquaintance," said she. "Being new here, I am in need of some assistance, and Mr. Rutherford advised me that you would be the best person to apply to."

"Mr. Rutherford?" said I, astonished. "I have hardly exchanged two words with Mr. Rutherford since he arrived in Highbury."

"Nevertheless," said she, "he knows you, and has assured me you would be quite excellent for my purpose."

"Ah," said I, "you have a girl you wish to place in my school? Unless something unexpected occurs, I fear I shall have no vacancies until next September. There is not a spare bed in the house."

"Oh no, it is not that," said she.

Well, dear Charlotte, you can imagine how perplexing I found this little mystery.

"How may I be of assistance, then?" I asked, quite overcome with curiosity.

She did not at once explain what she had come for. Before she could do *that*, she said, or could expect me to acquiesce in her request, it was only right that I should understand her circumstances and know something of the Pringle family first.

"All of you," said she, "who have long resided in Highbury, must know almost everything about each other. On the other hand my son and I, who have now come to live amongst you, are complete strangers. Is it not fair that you should learn something of us and our situation?"

I murmured something to the effect that in due time, etc. But she was determined to proceed, and I, I must admit, was not averse to hearing.

"My son and I," she began, "have taken Hartfield, furnished, for one year. If we like the neighbourhood, we may engage for a longer lease or possibly my son may purchase somewhere in the vicinity. I realize it may be difficult to accept newcomers occupying Hartfield and I understand Mr. John Knightley does not intend to settle here until he retires." She paused, and before I could disclaim, she remarked, "Charles Rutherford has told me that he heard from Mr. Perry you often visited the house."

I acknowledged that I had known the Woodhouse family for some seventeen years, and that I had owed much to Mr. Woodhouse's kindness when I had first come to Highbury and opened my school. While I was talking I was thinking to myself that Mrs. Pringle's frankness was quite disarming, and it made me respect her mightily. I saw that in spite of their supposed wealth, there was absolutely no pretension about her whatsoever. She then began to tell me about William Pringle, her only son. She said he had always been everything to her, but now she was a widow, he meant, if possible, even more.

"He is a good son to me," she said, "many young men of his age and independent means would not wish to live under the same roof as their mother. I want him to be happy here in Highbury. It is a great change for us to move from a town house in a large city to a country village and an estate such as Hartfield." She looked me straight in the face and smiled. "Mrs. Goddard, I will make no secret of the fact. We have been in trade. We have been living in Liverpool. I know it is a place of which people do not think much. I am told that in the south people despise Liverpool. But it would ill become me to say anything against the place in which the Pringles came by their fortune. They have been well-respected merchants there for several generations. But my husband, if you will excuse my saying so, made a very considerable sum of money. He valued this fortune because it enabled him to give William an education, such as he had never received himself. He sent him to a good school, and then on to Cambridge. William is the first of the family to attend one of the universities."

"Indeed?" said I.

"At Cambridge," she continued, "he was so fortunate as to make the acquaintance of Mr. Charles Rutherford. You may not know that Mr. Rutherford is a younger scion of a most respectable landed family also from the north. Had William not been at Cambridge he would never have met such a person as Mr. Rutherford."

"They are close friends, I understand?" said I, still wondering what this was leading up to and when she would come to the point.

"Yes. It is on account of this friendship that we have settled in Highbury. They say, do they not, Mrs. Goddard, that opposites attract? That is the case with my son and Mr. Pringle. The high spirits of one complements the more serious disposition of the other. Charles Rutherford is quite shy, you know, and fond of solitary, country pursuits. He likes to fish. Of course he also enjoys the exercise of hunting. Poor Charles! He would have done so well as a country gentleman, it is too bad he is obliged to earn his living. The priesthood can be quite a difficult profession, you know, especially for a young man who does not talk readily or meet people easily."

This remark, as you may imagine, Charlotte, gave me quite a different view of our lonely young vicar, one I would like to have explored further. "And you say they met at Cambridge?"

"Yes. Friendship with Charles Rutherford and invitations to the Rutherford estate, together with the three years he had spent at Cambridge gave William a distaste for the dirt and bustle of a city devoted to commerce. When Charles Rutherford was presented to the living here, he positively begged William to settle in Highbury. He put it to William that the green and pleasant south of England would be so much more agreeable than the black, industrial north. There was nothing to hinder us. My husband had died, and William had adequate means, and he had already determined on making a complete change of abode. It was all the same to him where he went. If Charles suggested Highbury, then Highbury it was. Quite as good a choice as any other place."

"Or even better," I said, smiling. "We who live here think there is nothing to surpass Highbury."

"That may be so," said she. "But these two young men have neither of them any acquaintance here."

"Ah," said I, glad of a chance to say something sensible at last. "I have been concerned for Mr. Rutherford. I knew he must be lonely and I wished it had been in my power to do something for him. But you understand, in a girls' school it is not easy to extend any sort of invitation to a single young man."

"Of course," said she, "and that is exactly what I have come about."

At last! I thought. She is coming to the point, whatever it is. She paused. "My son and I wish to give a ball at Hartfield."

"A ball!" I cried, astonished.

"Yes, a ball, and we would like you to draw up the list of guests to be invited."

"I!" I cried, in amazement.

"Yes. If you would be so kind. I know it seems very soon after our arrival," said she, "but it cannot be too soon for us to become acquainted with our neighbours."

"I would be glad to help," I said, slowly recovering myself, "but I do not believe I am at all the right person. I seldom leave the school grounds, I am not any leader of Highbury society. Mrs. Knightley at Donwell would be a much better choice. She would be the one to apply to."

"No . . ." Mrs. Pringle hesitated a moment, seemed to be choosing her words carefully. "I do not think Mrs. Knightley would do. William and I would like to ask—well, not just. . . ." —she paused again, smiled—"well, not what you yourself call society. I have told you, we have been in trade, we are not smart people, we would like to invite anyone in Highbury who would enjoy coming to Hartfield."

"Anyone!" I exclaimed, quite taken aback.

"Yes. Anyone. Everyone. Well, almost everyone."

It took me a moment, Charlotte, to realize the implications of this statement.

"Very few of the people of Highbury have ever been inside Hartfield," I ventured.

"I understand," said she, tactfully, "that Mr. Woodhouse's state of health had for some years precluded their entertaining."

"That is true," I replied. "He was quite an invalid."

"Then do you not think it an excellent plan?" said she.

"I think it is a plan that will give great satisfaction. People will be delighted to accept such an invitation."

"There you are then. That is exactly what William and Mr. Rutherford hoped you would say."

At that moment, Louisa and Lavinia Ludgrove walked into the room, not being aware (or perhaps they were—very much so) that I had a visitor. They apologised, curtseyed, dimpled prettily and went out again, leaving the door ajar behind them.

"What charming, pretty girls," cried Mrs. Pringle, "and as alike as two peas, I'll be bound. May we not be introduced?"

I went to the door and called them back. Of course they had not gone very far at all, were lurking in the passageway, ears cocked. "Girls," I said, "come back in. I would like you to meet this lady who is living at Hartfield. Mrs. Pringle, may I present my two parlour boarders, Louisa and Lavinia Ludgrove. You can tell them apart by their ribbons. Louisa wears green and Lavinia wears lavender."

The girls giggled and exchanged glances. Had they been changing those ribbons again, I wondered.

Mrs. Pringle was obviously bewitched.

"I hope these two can be at the top of the list," said she. "Pretty girls at a ball are an absolute necessity."

"A ball!" cried one, clapping her hands in joy.

"Where? When?" cried the other.

"At Hartfield. As soon as Mrs. Goddard can provide me with a list of guests," said Mrs. Pringle.

"Really?" said I. "So soon?"

"Why not? The sooner the better. We are lucky in having a very good cook, and I am sure she can produce an adequate supper without too much notice."

"Oh, Mrs. Goddard, may we help with the list?"

"Yes, yes, *please*, Mrs. Goddard, you can dictate to us, and we'll write out the names. It will save you so much trouble."

"Do let us, Mrs. Goddard. Our very best handwriting, we promise!"

"Very well," I said, knowing that I could accomplish the task much more effectively alone, but knowing, also, what pleasure it would give them. "We will do it together this evening."

Mrs. Pringle expressed gratitude, and we discussed details of possible numbers, music, supper, disposition of carriages, and, before she took her leave, a particular request from her to say nothing to anyone until the invitations were out.

"A frivolous conceit of mine, no doubt," said she, smiling at us, "but I would like to surprise the good people of Highbury."

We promised. I am sure with great reluctance on the girls' part, and she left.

So this evening, after dinner, we sat down in my parlour. I confess to being in some perplexity. Yet what Mrs. Pringle had said was clear enough. *Everyone* was to be included, people who had never set foot in Hartfield before. For a moment a vision of Mr. Woodhouse floated before my eyes, he who could not bear more than eight to dinner! Whatever would he say?

In fact, my dear Charlotte, so ingrained has been the habit of considering Mr. Woodhouse with everything to do with Hartfield, that even though he is dead and gone, I had rather to convince myself of the propriety of such an affair and my own part in it. I found I must play devil's advocate, and remind myself that we have all heard of noble lords, such as Lord Egremont, who invite their servants and tenants to feasts upon the lawn, where one understands "plum puddings and loaves are piled like cannon balls," and we think it nothing particularly out of the way. There is surely no more discrepancy in *that*, I told myself, than there is in the ordinary folk of Highbury meeting each other at Hartfield? It is certainly not what one is used to, this mixing of all sorts and conditions at a ball. Not that I anticipate any kind of *revolution* taking place, such as occurred in America and France when we were children. No. What I *hope* will happen is that these good people will come to Hartfield, be grateful and delighted to be admitted to its luxuries, and will the next day return to their allotted places in society. At least that is how I envision it. I hope my confidence is not misplaced, because think of the confusion, otherwise.

Thus was the list made out this evening. The twins' excitement was beyond anything as they transcribed the names, each taking a turn at a page. There was much giggling and cries of, "Oh, Mrs. Goddard!" with every person I proposed. One or two suggestions of their own were also brought forward. They had several times observed, parading about the High Street, a handsome ploughboy who works for Robert Martin, and suggested him, if you please. I told them Mrs. Pringle was not expecting to go quite that low. Of course they were teasing, or half-teasing me, and more laughter and giggles succeeded my refusal. At one point Miss Richardson opened the door, thinking from the noise that I was not present and the girls were up to some mischief. But having given our word to Mrs. Pringle we could not explain what we were up to, and I fear poor Miss Richardson went away quite offended.

You will not wish to hear the names of everyone who is to come, I am sure. But given your interest in Highbury affairs, for your information I will tell you that I made a point of including such worthy people as Robert Martin and Harriet, Mrs. Martin and Elizabeth, the whole Cox family, the two Gilberts, Mr. and Mrs. Perry (Mrs. Perry had never been inside the house, and he only in his professional capacity), the six Otways, Dr. and Mrs. Hughes (they were at the Westons' ball) and Mr. Richard Hughes, Mr. and Mrs. Cole (strangely enough, considering that Emma had been there for dinner, they had never been inside Hartfield, either), and all the upper tradespeople: Mrs. Stokes of the Crown, Mrs. Ford of the shop, and so on and so forth. I hope I have done right.

Such a responsibility! I am quite worn out. It is time I blew out my candle and went to bed.

Yours aff:ly,
Mary

P.S. Of course the Knightleys and the Westons are included, though I feel certain Emma will not come. How could she endure to do so?

(Mrs. Pinkney to Mrs. Goddard)

Hans Place
11 November 1816

Turning in his grave, I should think, Mr. Woodhouse is.

Imagine the ragtag and bobtail of Highbury hoofing it in Hartfield! Whatever will our Emma say? Suggest to Mr. J.K. that he cancel the lease at once, I should imagine. What an extraordinary state of affairs, my dear Mary. Yet I cannot help but be charmed with what you tell me of Mrs. Pringle. She seems a most agreeable woman, even if she does have rather strange notions. It is certainly a novel idea to ask *everyone* to her ball. I hope it will not throw the social life of Highbury into irredeemable disarray. At least she shows very good sense in appointing you arbiter of her list. It sounds to me as if things were likely to be rather lively in Highbury. It is a long time since you had a ball. Mrs. Weston's at the Crown was the last one, was it not?

Well! While you are expecting to dance, we are arranging to dine. This dinner party will be a very great event, though only two guests are to be invited—apart from the Captain, that is, who, of course, is already present. Am I tantalizing you? Whom do you imagine we are about to entertain? The Prince Regent? The Lord Mayor? The Duke of Wellington? Can you guess *why* this will be such a great occasion?

The reason is simple. The guests are to be the John Knightleys, and the John Knightleys *never* dine with anyone. It is his express wish. In the evenings he desires only to be alone with his wife and children. We, for example, have never been invited to Brunswick Square. My continuing friendship with Isabella is sustained entirely on morning calls and meetings in the park, sometimes by chance, sometimes by design. You may appreciate, therefore, the stratagems necessary to lure Mr. J.K. to Hans Place.

It is for Captain Gordon's sake. He, having no interest at the Admiralty and no acquaintances who could be of the smallest use to him, has met with absolutely no success in his attempts to obtain a pension or any recompense for the years he spent shipwrecked on that desert island. As he has been with us for six weeks now with nothing to show for it, and growing obviously more distressed every day, I decided it was high time to take matters into my own hands.

You have often heard me remark that I have never particularly liked what I knew of Mr. John Knightley, from hearsay only, of course. But here is an occasion when his connexions and his legal knowledge could be useful. I explained the case to Isabella, stressed how much Captain Gordon was in need, as well as deserving, of help, and begged her to do everything in her power to persuade her husband to accept the invitation. She replied that if he knew the reason he would definitely decline. It was a sacred tenet with him: never to do business in the evenings.

"Well, then," said I, "do not tell him the reason, but do, my dear Isabella, inveigle him here."

She was unwilling to deceive her husband, even in such a trifling matter as an invitation to dinner. But I assured her it was a most worthy and deserving cause, and with a great deal of reluctance she finally agreed to speak to him.

When she broached the subject, she made a point, as she told me later, of saying that to please *her*, since she and I were such particular friends and he had never met either me or Mr. Pinkney, would he consent to dine in Hans Place? We were not only friends, she reminded him, but there was also the Highbury connexion—so she really very much wished him to accept, *just this once*. She promised never to ask him to go out to dinner again.

She must have been very persuasive, for he has actually agreed to come. Friday, at the end of this week, is the fateful day. I think what particularly precipitated this endeavour was my inquiring of Captain Gordon the other evening after young Charlotte. I observed he did not appear to have received any letters from her, and I wondered if she was well. He looked fearfully embarrassed and said they thought they could save expense by not corresponding. This brought home to me his truly abject poverty, and I determined then and there to do for him whatever was in my power.

So, think of us, dear Mary, and hope for a favourable outcome.

Adieu,
Charlotte

P.S. I forgot to mention that Sophy came to dinner yesterday and seemed much as usual. In the light of your advice I did observe her with an especially scrutinizing eye—but to no particular purpose. If anything, she did not mention the man as frequently as she has done before.

Letter 33

(From Charlotte Marlowe to Captain Gordon)

Mrs. Smith's Lodgings
Portsmouth
12 November 1816

My dear Papa,

I am so happy to be able to send you a letter. How often I have rued our agreement not to write unless there was something of importance to impart. But the bearer of this will be his own explanation.

Lieutenant Chambers has just called in to say goodbye. He has been unexpectedly sent to London to report at Greenwich, or I would have been better prepared. I immediately asked him if he could wait five minutes and take a letter which I would hastily write. He readily assented and will deliver it himself in Hans Place. He was the more glad to do so since he says he once served under you. It was a long time ago, and perhaps you do not remember him?

He has been here in Portsmouth these last three weeks convalescing at the naval hospital, and being now pretty well recovered, is on his way to town. He and Richard were brother officers in the Anti-Slave Trade Squadron together, but Lieutenant Chambers was fortunate to escape from that vile duty. If you can call a badly broken leg fortunate. The surgeon on board said it would be months mending, so he was posted home. He is sitting reading the newspaper as I write.

The newspaper! No, dear Papa, I have not become wildly extravagant. It is not my paper, but his own he brought with him, and which he offers to leave behind when he goes. Whilst in Portsmouth he has called several times, and you can imagine how pleased I have been to hear at first hand news of Richard. It has been very agreeable to talk for a change to another adult person. He has kindly done various little jobs for me—mended that leg on the table which always gave us so much trouble and which made it stand unevenly. Then he repaired the larder door, which would never shut properly, and reinforced that shelf which was always so rickety. I like that term "brother officer." They really are *brothers* in their loyalty to each other and goodness to each others' families. Lieutenant Chambers seemed to like to visit here and after so long at sea to come into a *home*, as he said. (Even one as humble as ours!) He often played with little Richard while I was busy with the baby, and remarked how like his father he was, which pleased me mightily, as you may imagine.

You have been away a prodigious long time. I miss you, and hope you will be back soon. I am getting along better than I expected. Mrs. Smith has been more agreeable lately, and has at last offered to have that leaking window reglazed. As you suggested, in the end she would be obliged to do so, since the water was dripping through our floor and the ceiling into her own parlour below.

Little Lottie cries less than formerly. I have been giving her beef tea and a coddled egg. She seems to like it. Perhaps she was hungry before.

Lieutenant Chambers must now leave to catch the coach, so, alas, I have not time for more.

My dear father, I was so hoping your visit would prove prosperous, but your silence, and the age you have been gone leads me to suppose otherwise.

Ever your affectionate daughter,
Charlotte Marlowe

Letter 34

(From Mrs. Goddard to Mrs. Pinkney)

Highbury
12 November 1816

You know how highly I think of the Knightley family, my dear Charlotte, and I can understand Mrs. John Knightley's concern at deceiving her husband even in so small a matter. Perhaps she has read Scott:

> *O, what a tangled web we weave,*
> *When first we practise to deceive.*

What if it should ever come out later, in conversation, the true *raison d'être* of this dinner-party, supposedly given in a spirit of friendship? It would hardly encourage Mr. Knightley to respect and trust his wife in the future. But you will say I am too nice, too scrupulous. Unfortunately, I cannot rid myself of my years of being mistress of a school, and endeavouring to inculcate right principles in the young. Still, I hope the affair may have a happy resolution, and no doubt you are telling yourself that the end justifies the means.

As for this proposed ball at Highbury, you will be amused to hear that the next morning after we had made out the list, Louisa and Lavinia begged if they might themselves deliver it to Mrs. Pringle. I saw no reason why they should not, so after breakfast off they went.

They came back agog. The door was opened by no less a person than young Mr. William Pringle, himself. In spite of all the many servants! Perhaps he was glancing out of the window and saw them come through the great iron sweep gate and walk up the drive, and not being averse to making the acquaintance of two pretty girls, rushed to be the first to speak to them. That is only surmise, of course. At all events he had just arrived from town that very morning, and was delighted that his mother's plans for the ball were so far advanced.

Mrs. Pringle invited the girls to stay and have a cup of chocolate. So they sat in the morning room, and while she occupied herself at her tambour frame—with many an amused glance in their direction, as I understand it, the three young people engaged in some spirited banter. Mr. William Pringle was absolutely captivated by the twins (as they quite shamelessly told me). They are accustomed to being stared at by strangers because of their remarkable likeness to each other, but not often, or ever, by such a very eligible young man. There are not many such in Highbury. He asked them all the usual sorts of questions, which they have long been in the habit of answering.

"Was it not very strange to be a twin?"

"You get used to it, sir," replied Louisa, as she told me. "You look across a room and see yourself, or at least you realize you are looking at what other people see as either you, or your twin, and that they do not know which of you is which."

"Indeed?"

"And nothing can ever be *yours*," Lavinia explained to him.

91

"It must always be ours. *Our* hair is curly, *our* eyes are brown, *we* have dimples, *we* look best in white. You can never say *my*, not even of your own birthday."

"Extraordinary," said the young man, who had obviously never thought of such a thing. "Do you ever attempt to confuse people?"

"Oh, never," said Louisa.

"Louisa!" cried Lavinia.

"Well, sometimes," said Louisa. "It is rather diverting."

"For you, I imagine it might be."

"Do you want to know how we do it?" said Lavinia. "Mrs. Goddard resolved that at school we should wear different ribbons. I should wear lavender and Louisa should wear green."

"So, of course, you exchange?"

"Of course."

"And have you today?"

"Guess?"

"How can I guess?"

"You can try."

"And if you tell me you really are Miss Louisa who is wearing green, how do I know you are not jesting with me?"

"You'll have to take our word for it."

"And how trustworthy is your word?"

"That you will have to discover, sir."

This conversation the twins repeated to me with great glee, and volunteered quite shamelessly that Mr. Pringle was evidently so entranced he insisted on escorting them back to school.

I happened to be outside talking to John about cleaning the gutters when they came walking up to the gate, the three of them full of chat and good-humour and smiles.

Mr. Pringle was introduced. He is a handsome, lively young man, with a pleasant open countenance. He thanked me for providing the list of guests, and extended an invitation to call on his mother very soon. I might say that although he was ostensibly speaking to me, his eyes were fixed chiefly on the girls. I was much amused, and obviously must not neglect to take them with me when I go to Hartfield, which, however, I see no occasion for doing at present.

As soon as Mr. Pringle had walked out of the gate and the twins had come in and taken off their bonnets, this little tale came eagerly tumbling out of their mouths. I must say I like what I have heard and seen of the Pringles. I liked the young man in the few words we exchanged and I liked his answering the door himself. I fancied that his recent inheritance and his years at Cambridge had not made him vain or proud. Very amiable, unassuming people, the Pringles seem to be.

There, my dear Charlotte, how tame and trifling this little encounter must seem to you compared to your more serious troubles with Captain Gordon and Sophy.

Later: I had only got so far, when Miss Nash came in to say that last night two of the older girls were caught making apple pie beds in the younger girls' bedrooms, which caused some tears, and re-arrangement of sheets and bed clothing when everyone was tired and cross. A relatively venial offence, but I have had to call in the culprits and chide them. I do so hate unpleasantness.

Yours affect:ly
M. G.

Letter 35

(From Mrs. Pinkney to Mrs. Goddard)

Hans Place
Saturday

Unpleasantness? Apple pie beds. A young man opening the front door himself! My dear Mary, such great events in Highbury! How I envy you your paradise.

Well, last night the famous dinner party took place. I flatter myself you are interested in the occasion in spite of your rebuke as to the manner of its being brought about.

Mr. Pinkney and I had discussed our arrangements beforehand. We decided not to tell Captain Gordon too much or to indicate our hopes for the evening. He is such an honourable, forthright man, we thought if he knew of our plans he might be nervous, blurt something out and not present himself to best advantage.

So we simply told him that Mrs. Knightley was my particular friend and that Mr. John Knightley was a lawyer who sometimes did business at the Admiralty. He could make of that what he would.

When our guests came, it fell to Isabella to effect the introductions, since neither Mr. Pinkney nor I had ever met Mr. J.K. As I suspected, he has no small talk, and unless he can say something of importance will say nothing at all. On the other hand I was much impressed by Captain Gordon. He was no longer the humble and grateful guest we had entertained these many weeks, but became every inch a naval officer. His dignity and bearing I hoped could not fail to strike Mr. J.K. favourably.

At first the discourse was infinitely dreary, the weather, and, when that failed, a desultory account of the latest show at Astleys, to which the Knightleys are addicted to taking the older children. What is more tiresome, dear Mary, than listening to a description of an entertainment in which one has no interest and at which one has no intention of ever being present? I thought I would die of boredom and began quite to despair for the success of my party. Once Astleys was exhausted, even Isabella, so ready to talk when alone with me, fell silent. She is, one assumes, like many other wives I have observed retiring in company in the presence of her husband, deeming it unseemly in any way to put herself forward or to outshine her lord and master. This state of affairs continued for some time. But since two, if not three people at the table were well aware of the purpose of the evening—everybody, you might say, except the two principals—Mr. Pinkney and I bent every effort to channel the conversation in the right direction.

It was not until after the mutton had been carved, and Mr. P. had made several proposals of wine, which they, from civility, could hardly fail to acknowledge, that matters improved. Mr. Pinkney astutely began to ask Captain Gordon about his adventures—quite as if he had never heard them before. Who knows what Captain Gordon thought of this, but he did respond, as a good guest should for the entertainment of the company, by talking and describing the island on which they were shipwrecked.

At first, Mr. J.K. showed little curiosity, possibly he was lamenting his absence from home, and the loss of an evening with his children. Who knows? Captain Gordon with only a somewhat less-than-enraptured audience did not exhibit his usual flair for an anecdote. Eventually, however, Mr. John Knightley could not help but be caught up in the tale and to be struck by the drama of the story. After all, how often does one meet at a London dinner table a man who has spent three years on a desert island? Like any intelligent person must do, Mr. J.K. began to take an interest in circumstances which were entirely new to him. No doubt he had been obliged to drink more wine than he wished, but Mr. P. and I were delighted to see him finally leaning forward, almost eagerly encouraging Captain Gordon to tell him more particularly the details of the contrivances they employed in order to survive. I caught Isabella's eye, though she instantly looked away, beset by her guilty conscience, perhaps? Captain Gordon, with the wine and the attention, quite rose to the occasion. I've always found sailors to be excellent raconteurs. I suppose they have to pass the time somehow or other on a passage. He told how the castaways had found a few seeds in the wreckage of the ship, and how they planted and cultivated them, so that by the third year of their solitude they had quite a respectable crop of wheat. He also described how they kept track of time by cutting into a log with a knife the date of each day that passed. Mr. John Knightley asked many questions such as what protection they had from the elements, and was told how they constructed a shelter out of an old sail and some timbers that had washed ashore. All this, of course, Mr. Pinkney and I have heard before, but I like to fancy that we gave every indication of listening to the story for the first time.

After dinner we two ladies repaired to the drawing-room for coffee, leaving the men to their port. Isabella was gently happy for my sake that the evening seemed to be going well, but still had some regrets that she had inveigled her husband here under what she deemed false pretences. Dear Isabella! She has no equal.

It was a long time, a very long time, before the three gentlemen emerged. Later, Mr. Pinkney told me he led the conversation round to the shocking way sailors were often treated, even after enduring great hardships in the line of duty, and cited Captain Gordon and Captain George Vancouver as examples. He said that Mr. John Knightley on being apprised of Captain Gordon's present circumstances was greatly indignant and offered at once to speak to an acquaintance in the Admiralty. You can imagine our relief that the whole purpose of this deceiving dinner was thus to be realised.

I had a note from Isabella this morning. She said her husband had found the evening most interesting and observed that he did not often have a chance to talk to someone outside his own profession. Well, of course he does not, since he refuses to go out into society.

How I hope, both for Captain Gordon's sake and our own, that Mr. John Knightley's application is successful. Captain Gordon is not in any way an unpleasant guest, in fact quite the reverse, but naturally Mr. Pinkney's and my conversation is constrained at meals when he is sitting with us at the table. Our evenings, too, are not our own. We would be happy to be alone together again in our house with our little boy.

Ever yours,
Charlotte Pinkney

Letter 36

(From Mrs. Goddard to Mrs. Pinkney)

I trust Mr. John Knightley's undertaking will come to something, my dear Charlotte. Not, that he would not do what he promised, in *this* instance, I feel sure, (in spite of his not turning up for the move to Donwell). But still, results must be dependent on the goodwill of others over which he can have no control.

The invitations to the ball have not yet been received. I am not sure why there is this delay. My silly girls expected they would arrive the next day, and here is a whole week gone by. They keep begging me to call on Mrs. Pringle and take them along with me, pointing out that William Pringle invited me to do so. I tell them I am too busy to spare the time. But the truth is I do not feel it would be at all appropriate thus to put myself forward. And what would we talk about if not the ball? I can hardly ask my would-be hostess why the invitations have not been received. But the poor girls! It is quite an agony for them to remain mum on the subject. In the evening, when we are alone in my parlour, they give full vent to their feelings on the subject, alternating between black despair that there might never be any ball, and sanguine expectations of the bliss to be experienced when the glorious day, or should I say evening, actually dawns.

They have seen Mr. William Pringle only at church and *en passant* in the High Street and have had no opportunity, as they inform me, to ask him when the ball is to be, since there are always other people about and it is supposedly, in fact *is*, a secret. They expressed their disappointment that after such a brilliant first encounter, he has not been to call, or made any occasion for seeing them again.

"Do not fret yourselves," I tell them, "you will meet at the ball."

"If it ever happens," they reply gloomily.

"My dears," said I, "it is unfortunately the way of the world. I am afraid you must learn that men often have other interests. Women, in general, do not. Mr. Pringle is no doubt very busy about something or other."

My supposition proved correct. I heard later from Mrs. Cole that plans for starting up a hunt in Highbury have been going forward, and he and Mr. Rutherford have been running about the village interviewing anyone who might be willing to board out one of more of the hounds, which are due to arrive shortly. Well, I suppose a few more dogs lying about the street will make not much difference, and it will be easily earned extra income for the likes of John Abdy and the ostlers from the Crown.

Meantime, the twins are practising vigorously at a duet by Mozart with which they hope to astonish the company on the famous evening—if, as they say, it ever takes place. They have collected for their quotation books all that they can find on Romance and Love, and, deciding on an opposite tack, have now determined to explore the possibilities of Despair and Hope. I am rather amused.

Everything else at the school, outwardly at least, goes on as usual. The old writing master is as irascible as ever, but the girls do learn from him to write a pretty hand so I must put up with his ill-humour. You remember my former parlour boarder, Miss Bickerton, married his son? The music master, a much more tractable person, is pleased with the progress of the two little Cole girls who have begun at school with me this year. Since they have such a very superior grand piano at home, I am glad he has promoted them off the old spinet to the Broadwood, kept for the best pupils. It, of course, is the famous instrument given anonymously by Frank Churchill to Jane Fairfax, and generously presented by her to me on her marriage.

I can write no more. The younger children are skipping outside my window. It is a happy sound, and I would not stop it for the world, but with,

Benjamin Franklin went to France
To teach the ladies how to dance
First the heel, and then the toe,
Spring around and out you go.

ringing in my head, how can I possibly concentrate?

Yrs. aff:ly,
M. Goddard

P.S. Is Sophy getting along any better? I had rather a distressing meeting with Patty in the High Street the other day. She is now married to one of Mr. Cole's servants—the one with whom she used to rendezvous at the post office until she was denied that daily meeting when Jane Fairfax insisted on collecting their letters herself. I asked Patty if she had heard from Miss Bates, and she said she had had only one short note, and that it did not sound at all like her usual self. My poor old friend. I cannot get her out of my thoughts.

Letter 37

(From Captain Gordon to Charlotte Marlowe)

Hans Place
19 November 1816

My dear Lottie,

Thank you for yours, which I was extremely glad to have received. I have the opportunity of a frank by courtesy of a friend of Mr. Pinkney—a member of parliament. It was Mrs.

Pinkney who arranged this. She asked how you were getting along and was concerned we did not appear to be corresponding. So, for this exchange of letters, we are both indebted to the kindness of friends.

I had forgot young Chambers, he was only a very young mid in a ship I commanded many years ago. But when he walked into the drawing room, here, he recognized me at once, in spite of my grey locks. We had a very pleasant little recollection of past times, but more particularly I was pleased to hear a first-hand report of you and the little ones.

I said I would not write unless I had good news. This letter is really premature, because I have only the hope of good news, and were I as superstitious as most sailors I would not even be mentioning it. But I wanted to send you a word. Of course you have been wondering what has happened. I will admit I have been quite discouraged. Who could have foretold I would be gone so long, and with such little result? Mrs. Pinkney kindly invited to dine here on Friday her particular friend, a Mrs. John Knightley, and her husband. Knightley is a lawyer who has connexions at the Admiralty. In the course of the evening I was able to state my case. He was properly incensed on my behalf and has promised to speak for me in high quarters. He seems to be a man of integrity and likely to keep his word. I pray something may come of this for more reasons than the very obvious one of necessity.

Mr. and Mrs. Pinkney have been most agreeable, but they are a very devoted couple, and I am definitely *de trop*. I feel sure they would like to see me gone and to have their house to themselves. I try to keep out of the way as much as possible and go for long walks in the London streets, but I have not funds to lounge about in coffee houses, so these dark evenings I am obliged to return to Hans Place. I would often prefer to sit quietly and read—Mr. Pinkney has a very fine library—but they seem to enjoy a game of cards and I must do my duty.

If nothing comes of Knightley's speaking to his acquaintance, I shall be really in a poor way, as no other avenues appear to be open to me. I would very much dislike the thought that Mr. and Mrs. Pinkney had given me hospitality for so long in vain. But I must face the unpleasant possibility that I may have to return to Portsmouth as penniless as I left it.

I do very often think of you and wonder how you are managing, so I was very glad to hear of your various small victories on the domestic front. It seems young Chambers is a better carpenter than I am! I hope little Richard and little Lottie have not forgot their fond grandfather.

Ever your most aff. father,
A.J.G.

Letter 38

(From Mrs. Pinkney to Mrs. Goddard)

Hans Place
22 November 1816

I am glad to say there is hope for Captain Gordon, my dear Mary. An initial introduction has been effected with some important personage at the Admiralty, following which, investigations have taken place, and applications have been made. He remains with us, however, for the present. He does not choose to leave London until he has the promised pension actually in his hand. He is cautious, he has too often been disappointed by false promises to believe that it *will* be so until it *is* so. We continue to be gracious. We do not want to imply we wish him gone—because no guest could be less trouble. It is just that we prefer no guest at all.

I have not said much about Sophy, because there has been nothing new or cheerful to say, and I did not feel it was a subject worth writing about. But since you particularly ask, there has been no word from Barbadoes. I hear there have been bad storms in the Atlantic, which have no doubt delayed any ship bound for home. Sophy continues as resentful as ever. Last Sunday it was a frosty night, we had the fire going, our chairs drawn round. Somehow or other, the conversation got upon flogging, of all the extraordinary and disagreeable subjects. I think it began with a discussion of a report in the newspaper. A starving eight-year-old boy had stolen an apple and was sentenced to ten lashes, in the course of which he collapsed. We all agreed that it was an excessive punishment.

"Barbarous!" cried Mr. Pinkney warmly. "I do not believe that it should ever be necessary to flog anyone. I do not approve of it, whether it be thieving miscreants, or Negro slaves, or Eton schoolboys."

"Or sailors," said Captain Gordon unexpectedly. "I am proud that no sailor was ever flogged under my orders. Although regulations sometimes prescribed it as punishment for a particular offence, I always found a way around it."

"You feel strongly, evidently?" said Mr. Pinkney.

"I do. When I was a mid, a sailor on board our ship was ordered to be Flogged Round the Fleet. It made the greatest impression on me."

"What does that mean, sir?" asked Sophy.

"The sailor is taken in a boat to each ship at anchor. At each ship he is publicly flogged. It is supposed to be an example to others. A doctor is sent with him."

"A doctor?"

"It is the intention that he will stop the flogging when the man can stand no more."

"And does he?" I inquired.

"Rarely."

"What became of that sailor?" asked Sophy fearfully.

"He died, of course," said Captain Gordon, shortly. "I knew the man. His crime did not deserve such a punishment. He had a wife and children at home and there were extenuating circumstances which were never investigated. I vowed then and there that if ever I rose to command a ship, flogging should never take place aboard any vessel of mine."

This led Sophy (who has no idea of holding back and letting the older people take the lead in a conversation) to talk again of the Negroes in Barbadoes. She waxed quite indignant about the way they are used, citing instances of slaves who had served their masters faithfully and loyally for years, then, for the most trivial offence, on a whim, would be sentenced to fifty lashes, which they had to accept kneeling down in penitence.

To change this most unfortunate subject, I said presumably all slaves were not so treated, and I asked Sophy to tell us about her black Mammy, a favourite topic with her. This she did at some length, describing what a beautiful voice she had when she sang, and how kind and comforting she always was. Do you know, Mary, the child became quite a different person when talking in this way, softer, more sympathetic, altogether more captivating and attractive.

I was considering what a pity it was that she was not more often like this, which presumably was how she comported herself at home, when Captain Gordon remarked that Barbadoes always got the pick of the slaves, since, owing to the winds the traders arrived there first, and he inquired if this Negro woman had come over on a slave ship.

"Oh no, sir. She was born in Barbadoes and so was her mother. Her grandmother was the one who was brought from Africa. There had been a war between tribes. The grandmother was captured, and sold to a trader from Bristol in exchange for some bolts of cloth. She told this to her daughter, who told it to my Mammy, who told me."

"You can see that Sophy is very fond of this . . . person," I explained to Captain Gordon, being unsure quite how to refer to her.

"She brought me up," said Sophy simply. "I was only eight when my mother died. I do so wish she could read and write," she sighed, "then I could send her letters and hear from her."

"It would be a comfort, I am sure," said Mr. Pinkney, kindly.

"Well, soon you will see her again. The time will pass quickly."

"Not quickly enough," said Sophy, "and if my father decides to move back to England, I will never see her or my beloved Barbadoes again."

"Well, well," said Mr. Pinkney. "That is not definitely settled. He has talked of it before, and nothing has come of the proposal."

On this not very satisfactory note, the conversation ended.

Adieu,
Charlotte

P.S. I hope your ball will not be cancelled, that would be too desperately disappointing for your young people. But surely, after such enthusiastic planning on the part of Mrs. Pringle it is more likely than not to take place?

Letter 39

(From Mrs. Goddard to Mrs. Pinkney)

Highbury
23 November 1816

My dear Charlotte,

Thank goodness mine is a girls' school. I could not bear to be a dame at a boys' school and to have to dress the wounds inflicted by cruel masters on their pupils. I knew a woman once who had had to do that at Rugby, and extremely disagreeable she found it.

I am very sorry that Sophy continues miserable, and that nothing can be done for her. Once again, how trivial and happy are our little doings compared to your more serious worries.

Today, the invitations to the ball have finally been received by the inhabitants of Highbury. I am sure there are very many astonished households, and tongues a-buzzing. As you know, Mrs. Pringle had enjoined us not to mention the subject to anyone. I very much doubted if Louisa and Lavinia would be able to contain the momentous news. It would have been most natural to disseminate such interesting information to their schoolfellows. But they promised, and I am proud to say they kept their word. They are presently rejoicing in the well-earned pleasure of being able to inform everyone that they have known all about it, all along, and explaining to Miss Richardson (my three teachers have also been invited) why we were making so much noise in my parlour that evening.

After my own invitation had arrived this morning, I thought I should finally call on Mrs. Pringle. *Now*, I felt it would be entirely appropriate. I went about noon. Louisa and Lavinia were having their music lesson, so I was not obliged to take them with me. As I walked up to Hartfield, I was pleased and surprised to see the Knightley carriage at that moment driving out of the sweep. The carriage stopped and Emma let down the window. Civil pleasantries were exchanged, I inquiring after her little boy and how they were all settling in at Donwell, she regretting that since the card parties at Hartfield were no more, she seldom saw me these days. As she drove off, and I stood waiting for the front door to be opened, I reflected to myself that Emma is now entering in on her marriage proper, and it must be very pleasant to have only her husband to consider after the first two strenuous years which she and Mr. Knightley spent at Hartfield. It is a very great credit to the good feelings of all that it went so smoothly. Whenever the Bateses and I were there, I observed Mr. Woodhouse looking as comfortable as possible.

I was shown into the morning room by the Pringles' butler. There I found Mrs. Pringle seated at her desk. She greeted me in a most friendly manner and remarked that Mrs. Knightley had just called to thank her for the invitation, but as she was still in mourning, she was unable to accept. Mrs. Knightley, said

Mrs. Pringle, was very gracious and declared it was such a pleasure for her to visit the old familiar rooms again. This is what she *said*, though I have a suspicion that exactly the reverse is more likely to be the case. But Emma Woodhouse nearly always *said* the right thing, whatever her true feelings might be. Except, of course, on the famous occasion when she was rude to Miss Bates at Boxhill, as reported to me by Harriet. But that is long in the past. I believe she is greatly improved by marriage. That is if one allows that there was any room for improvement! She certainly looked very blooming.

It was a strange experience for me to find myself inside Hartfield for the first time since the Woodhouses lived there. Since it is let furnished, the furniture is largely that which was there before, though Mrs. Pringle has added some things of her own. Expensive Wedgwood vases stand about on small tables, new pictures—mostly of stags and sheep—ornament the walls, some of the carpets and curtains have been changed, and different servants answer the door and bring the tea. She says she likes the house very much. It is well-built and convenient and Highbury is such a cheerful place after Liverpool.

"Of course," said she, "I must face the fact that I may not be able to live here for long. My dear William could very likely be married soon."

"Really, madam," said I, quite taken aback, for I was thinking of the twins, "has he someone in view?"

"Oh, no, not at all. But young men in general, you know, do get married, and it does not hurt to be prepared, because then I shall have to think what I shall do. I would not want to stand in his way. A small house nearby, so that I could see my grandchildren, would perfectly satisfy me. Lately, however, William has been much occupied with the business of purchasing a cry of hounds. Now he is trying to arrange to board them out with whomever will take them."

"So I have heard," I replied. "We have not had hounds in Highbury before."

"Of course William has no experience of such things, himself," said his mother, "but Mr. Rutherford is very keen, he is helping him manage it all. It is a good arrangement. William provides the funds and Charles the knowledge. It is a sport they can enjoy together."

"Indeed?" said I. "Will our vicar be keeping hunters then?"

"Oh, no," she said, quite shocked. "Hunters are very expensive and Charles Rutherford has no money at all. No, the pack will be harriers, the men will follow the hounds on foot and hunt hares. They carry long poles, I'm told, to help themselves over hedges and ditches. In Liverpool we knew nothing of such things, but I mentioned the matter to Mrs. Knightley and she thought Mr. Knightley would quite approve. I have been in Highbury long enough, Mrs. Goddard, to understand that Mr. Knightley's approval is very important."

"Ah yes, it is indeed," said I, amazed by her shrewdness.

"Mrs. Knightley said that Mr. Knightley often mentioned that there were too many hares hereabouts. A positive plague. They quite ravage the crops."

I was struck by the simple reality of the circumstance compared to the extravagant gossip which had preceded this plan of hunting, when rumour had conjured up a vision of a dozen horses, mounted by riders in hunting pink, galloping through the town in reckless pursuit of a fox.

"I have heard," I said, "that some people are beginning to think the clergy ought not to hunt."

"Ah," said Mrs. Pringle, "the Evangelicals. I gather there are none of those in Highbury. I think only good can come of a young man getting outside into the open air and taking some exercise. If he does not neglect his duties, what harm can it do to his congregation?"

I did not feel equal to entering into any kind of debate on the subject, and the conversation soon turned to details of the ball. She has engaged two musicians to come down from London to play for the dancing. It was the difficulty of securing *them* that caused the delay in sending out the invitations. While I was with her, the door bell was constantly ringing with notes of acceptance pouring in.

As I walked home I encountered many happy smiles along the way. I called in at Ford's, thinking I may as well purchase some new gloves for the ball before everybody else had the same notion. Mrs. Ford, who has few treats or pleasures in her hard-working life, was beaming with delight.

"Oh, Mrs. Goddard," cried she, "just fancy! Did you know there is to be a ball at Hartfield and we are all invited?"

Further along the road I encountered Mr. Rutherford, who tipped his hat to me and observed that his friend William Pringle was most grateful for the help I had given his mother.

I was about to say something graceful to the effect that the pleasure I had in so doing, was nothing to the pleasure anticipated by the whole of Highbury, when at that very moment, before I could open my lips, there appeared (it could almost have been out of an invisible hole in the ground) the twins, presenting their beaming faces to me, and standing there, most obviously waiting for an introduction. Since Mr. Rutherford did not look unwilling, this I performed. Two curtseys and a bow succeeded. Mr. Rutherford remarked that his friend Mr. Pringle had told him that he had already met the Miss Ludgroves, and he himself had noticed them in church, and which twin was which? The usual explanations and remarks followed, green and lavender, etc.

While they were thus talking, Elizabeth Martin came walking along the Donwell Road, also intending, I felt sure, to pay a visit to Ford's. Being a modest young woman, she would have passed by on the other side without stopping had I not called out to her, and made her come over and be introduced. She is not as pretty or as *showy* as Louisa and Lavinia, but she has a pleasant, sensible face, and a character which is more likely to endure than the transient charms of the twins. The young people, with the common interest of the ball, soon grew animated, talking of the prodigious pleasure they expected to derive from the occasion.

I stood there, amused, listening. I was perfectly aware that they all wished me gone. But the longer I stayed, the longer Elizabeth remained. I knew she would leave, if I did. I confess I enjoyed watching them. Eventually Mr. Rutherford with evident reluctance said he really must go. He had a meeting to attend on parish business and must not keep Mr. Knightley and Mr. Cole and Mr. Weston waiting.

"If you are going to the Crown," said I, "perhaps you would be so good as to accompany Miss Martin as far as Ford's."

"We will come, too!" cried the twins eagerly.

"No, my dears," said I. "I want you at home."

Mr. Rutherford and Elizabeth set off together along the High Street. The twins with a very good grace walked with me back to the school, but were so full of giggles and nudgings of elbows that even I was almost out of patience.

Yours aff:ly,
M. Goddard

Letter 40

(From Mrs. Pinkney to Mrs. Goddard)

Hans Place
Sunday 24 November 1816

Your Louisa and Lavinia sound enchanting, my dear Mary. I fear that Elizabeth Martin will be out of luck, in spite of your manoeuvres. I believe young men are only too apt to choose beauty and vivacity before sense and virtue. I conjecture Elizabeth, worthy farm daughter that she is, is no match for them.

If Mr. Rutherford and Mr. Pringle are not already violently in love with the twins, without doubt they soon will be.

It now appears that Captain Gordon will definitely receive the pension which is his due. I must give all credit to Mr. John Knightley in this business, he espoused Captain Gordon's cause as warmly as if it were his own. I begin to understand why Isabella is devoted, given her nature. A man with such reserved manners, however, would not suit me. Yes, dear Mary, I must retract some of my former opinions. Still, in general I do not find Mr. J.K. easy. He may be clever, he may be honourable, but he is not congenial. Well, well, we must possess ourselves in patience a few more days before the papers are finally signed. Meanwhile, Captain Gordon remains here. If only Sophy were less unhappy, we would have nothing left to wish for.

You have a ball in prospect, *we* also have a social occasion which promises well. An old friend of Mr. Pinkney from his former college at Oxford has been elected Member for the University. He has come up to town to take his seat in Parliament and has already been to call on us. The week after next a grand *soirée* is to be given in honour of Mr. Falconbridge. All London will be there. All London? Do I hear objections from my literal-minded sister? Well, you know very well what I mean, and do not scold me, dear Mary. I am not in any danger of fawning on great people. But I do enjoy society, of which, owing to Captain Gordon, we have had too little of late. I delight in hearing brilliant conversation and being in company with elegant women and clever, well-informed men. My chief concern is what I shall wear on this grand occasion. Betty and I have been through my wardrobe and concluded that I must have a new gown. Mr. Pinkney remarked that *that* conclusion was absolutely foregone, whether we had spent a morning looking through my clothes or not. But he is perfectly agreeable and has told me to choose what I like. Dear man! Tomorrow Betty and I go to Sackville Street, where Isabella tells me one of the linen drapers has some very pretty figured muslin at seven shillings a yard.

I am greatly looking forward to this party. I declare I am almost in as much of a flutter as I daresay Louisa and Lavinia are in anticipation of the ball.

Adieu,
Charlotte

Letter 41

(Mrs. Suckling to Mrs. Elton)

Maple Grove
nr. Bristol
Tuesday

My dear Augusta,

It is too, too vexatious. You will have received, by now, the express we sent on Sunday. We are prodigiously provoked. Who could have foreseen that a wheel would come off? Luckily we were not badly hurt, only bruised and tumbled about together on our sides against the door, Mr. Suckling receiving a sharp blow when the carriage clock flew off its bracket and struck him on the shoulder. It was a most disagreeable experience, I assure you. I blame James. He should have made certain that all was in order and inspected the barouche-landau thoroughly before we left Bristol. He makes the excuse that it was an exceptionally large hole in the road we fell into. However that may be, the axle broke and we had to return home with my maid, our sheets and our trunks all in a hired coach. Very unpleasant, indeed. We left James and the barouche-landau behind at Petty France, where he is to see to its repair.

Having had this misadventure, Mr. Suckling is not in the mood to set forth again at present. In fact, between you and me, he was quite put out on the occasion. What we women have to endure! Anyone would think it had been *my* fault.

I shall have to take comfort in my works in the garden.

I am quite out of countenance and in no mood to write more.

Yours aff:
Selina Suckling

Letter 42

(From Mrs. Elton to Mrs. Suckling)

St. Stephen's Rectory
Arabella Street
London
27 November 1816

My dear Selina,

Upon my word, I would not have had this happen for any consideration. I will not conceal from you that I was excessively annoyed when your express came. Not that you could have *foreseen* or *prevented* such a mishap, and I am thankful that none of you suffered any injury, but I had made arrangements for your entertainment which it has been awkward, not to say *mortifying* to rescind.

Sir Percival and Lady Lushley, members of our congregation, people of consequence—they move in the first circle—were to come and dine with us yesterday on what would have been your second evening here. Sir Percival had expressed *particular* interest in meeting Mr. Suckling. He is a member of one of the most important guilds in the city. He wishes to establish connexions in Bristol, I believe with some idea of furthering his own trade there. Since I had planned an intimate and elegant dinner-party of six only, I felt obliged to send a note to Lady Lushley informing her of your accident. She returned a letter of excuse, regretting she was indisposed, etc. etc. I saw all too plainly that they did not think it worth while coming to the rectory to meet only ourselves, whom they can see any Sunday at church.

Since the preparations had already been made and the food bought and needing to be cooked, and as I could not in decency invite anyone else at such short notice, I was obliged to ask Philip's mother and sisters. I believe they enjoyed themselves. They kept exclaiming at the good dinner, and asking Philip if this was how he ate every day. So vulgar.

It was a poor substitute, my dear Selina, for you and the Lushleys and our elegant party.

Your most disappointed sister,
Augusta Elton

Letter 43

(From Mrs. Goddard to Mrs. Pinkney)

Highbury
26 November 1816

I am glad, my dear Charlotte, that you have an evening party, this occasion for Mr. Falconbridge, to look forward to. With all the worries you have had lately you deserve a little plea-sure as well as a new gown. Let us hope for both yours and Cap-tain Gordon's sake that he will soon be gone from your house.

I am not ready as yet to discount Elizabeth Martin's chances. A young man with any intelligence, especially one in the clerical profession, ought to realize what a very superior wife she would make. Mr. Rutherford may be in a slightly higher rank in society than she is, but, unfortunately, belonging to the landed gentry is not much to the purpose if one has not the resources to support one's position. Any hope of his meeting an heiress in Highbury is absolutely non-existent. Besides, a good, sensible wife who can help with the parish duties would be infinitely more valuable, and more likely to ensure their future and lasting happiness, than some young woman of fortune and the pretensions that often accompany it. I do not quite like your calling Elizabeth a "worthy farm daughter." Her father was a decent gentleman farmer, and she has pleasant agreeable good manners that would be acceptable anywhere, and, furthermore, though I say it myself, an education from this school which is most adequate, if not superior, compared to that possessed by most of the people of Highbury. She is not entirely penniless. I believe she has £200 from a grandfather, and her *merit*, as a wife, would be beyond any mere pecuniary calculation.

If only the young had *wisdom!* You will say this sounds just like a schoolmistress, but it does trouble me that Mr. Rutherford could make a most grievous error. I cannot bear that good sense should be passed over in favour of youthful beauty and high spirits. Not that the twins are not very agreeable, good-natured girls, but at present they are too flighty and too young even to think of marriage.

Speaking of which, today I received a rude shock while making the Christmas puddings. (I am hoping very much, of course, that you and Mr. Pinkney and your little treasure will be here to help us eat them.) All morning my cook Sarah and I were busy about this task, which I have never been so tardy about tackling before, but the school has been so active with such a multitude of girls that Sarah and I have not been able to get at it sooner. It is our mother's receipt. You remember it? It makes a nice, rich, black pudding, which I have made every year since I was married. On this occasion, I fear it is almost too late for them to mature properly, and to assist that process I have put in a double quantity of brandy. I was amused that both the twins and little Sukey managed to insinuate themselves into the kitchen at the crucial moment, and were all pleased to drop in the sixpences as well as each to give a lucky stir to the batter. I asked them what they wished for, but not surprising, none of them would tell me. The twins, I must say, were rather endearing and not yet so grown-up that they were not just as eager as Sukey to join in licking off the spoons.

Goodness me, I seem to have wandered off from what I was going to tell you. You are no doubt asking yourself, where, pray, is the shock in a Christmas pudding, unless it be not properly cooked, and the sixpence turns out to be a plum stone?

Well, I thought Sarah was unusually cheerful while we were cutting up the fruit and chopping the suet and so on. After the girls had gone and the kitchen maids were tying up the puddings in their cloths and placing them in the large iron pot to boil, she drew me aside into the larder and informed me that she and John are intending to get married. I was so taken aback, I had to sit down and be given a cup of tea.

Sarah and John are each in their different way so essential to the successful running of this school, I cannot imagine its subsisting without them. When I had recovered somewhat, Sarah informed me that they wish to continue in my employment but would like to live outside the school, if they can find a suitable cottage nearby. I must now consider what arrangements can be made, and how Sarah not living in will affect the meals. John, too, for that matter, for in an emergency he has always been readily at hand, in his loft above the stables.

You will wonder how this announcement could so take me unawares. But neither of them is young, and I have never observed any signs of affection between them. Apparently the first flicker of any interest between them occurred the day of the chimney fire. Very strange. Perhaps it was John's heroic efforts on the roof. Thus more than the chimney was ignited! Sarah is an excellent cook, but like all good cooks, she is often in a bad temper. John is a loyal and faithful servant and a hard worker, but I have known him to be sullen and moody if things are not going as he expects. Well, well, they have worked here together these past five years, and all this must be known to each other.

I trust and believe Sarah is beyond child-bearing age.

Aff:ly,
M. Goddard

Letter 44

(From Mrs. Pinkney to Mrs. Goddard)

27 November 1816

I offer you my condolences, my dear Mary. Although I commiserate with you, I should in truth rejoice with Sarah. Please send her my felicitations if she remembers me.

Do you suppose the twins, when they gave their ceremonial stir of the Christmas pudding, each wished for the same handsome husband and ten thousand a year? One question you did not explore in your account of L. and L. is how any young man can tell them apart sufficiently to choose one to marry.

Speaking of Christmas puddings, by the bye, and while I have it in mind, quite aside from Mr. P.'s objections on Edward's account, which I believe to be insurmountable, I fear there is another reason why we cannot begin to entertain any idea of coming to you. Sophy. It would be quite impossible to leave her at the seminary for the holidays. Equally impossible, also, to bring her with us. She would be no asset at Highbury, merely dampen the spirits and spoil Christmas for everyone else. Presumably we will have to have her to stay here. I confess I dread the thought.

We have heard from her father at last. This, in answer to Mr. Pinkney's of September. Mr. Adams is determined. He says that since he knows nothing of Mr. Pinkney's wife's sister's school, and since he had an excellent report of Madame Dubois from Mr. and Mrs. Blair, he wishes Sophy to remain where she is. If she is a little bit unhappy, it is not long to suffer, and when he comes next July he will look forward to listening to her play the harp.

This discouraging news we had to relate to Sophy when she came as usual on Sunday. We were prepared for all sorts of scenes and tantrums, but she was not as put out as we thought she might be, which surprised us. She merely replied that she supposed one school was as bad as another. As usual she ate heartily, though her mind appeared abstracted. Her misery does not seem to have affected her appetite. One of us made a comment to the effect that we were glad she had enjoyed the pudding, which was a trifle, with a high whipped syllabub on top, and of which she dispatched three helpings. (Do you remember how we used to love trifle when we were young?) Even as Mr. Pinkney was laughing about it, and saying it was his favourite pudding, also, suddenly Sophy interrupted him, speaking so earnestly as to stop him in mid-sentence.

"Do you think, sir," said she, her eyes gazing straight into his, "that you could let me have five pounds?"

"Five pounds!" exclaimed Mr. Pinkney, taken aback, for he knows she has an adequate allowance.

"I need it for food," she said.

"For food?"

"For extra food?"

"I suppose the girls buy tuck, do they?" said Mr. Pinkney. "At school I remember spending most of my money on my stomach."

"They are certainly very ill-fed by that woman," I remarked.

"Yes," said Sophy, "very ill."

"But five pounds is a great deal of money for a young lady." said Mr. Pinkney.

"I know it," said she quite brazenly. "Have no fear. I will

117

see that my father repays you when he comes."

"That is not what I meant, young lady," said Mr. Pinkney, somewhat piqued, for he would do and does do everything he can for his sister's child.

If I had been he, I would not have given it to her. Nevertheless, since we had by now finished dinner, he went off to his room to fetch the money, which luckily he happened to have on hand. Sophy and I and Captain Gordon remained in an uncomfortable silence in the dining-room. One cannot imagine why she should want such a sum, and later, after Captain Gordon had retired, I asked Mr. P. why he had given it to her.

"Well, my dear," said he, "the girl is so miserable. I hate to deny her. If she can buy herself any little comforts with this extra money, I am glad that she should have it."

"Little comforts!" said I, "she will be able to quite pamper herself."

Then I remembered how he had given young Charlotte five guineas at Bath three years ago, and I had not objected, in fact I had applauded his generosity. But that was a gift, and Charlotte was poor. This was a flagrant petition, and Sophy is not poor. Well, I thought, it is his niece and his money.

"You are a kind soul, my love," I said stretching out my hand to him, "come to bed."

And he did.

Ever yours,
Charlotte

Letter 45

(From Mrs. Goddard to Mrs. Pinkney)

Highbury
28 November 1816

Five pounds! That is what I pay Daisy, my youngest kitchen maid, for an entire year. What can she want with such a sum? I hope Sophy does not intend it for some nefarious purpose, my dear Charlotte. I would keep an eye on her, if I were you. It is unfortunate, though understandable, that her father does not wish her to change schools. I suppose Mr. Adams cannot comprehend from such a distance the real implications of her situation. Alas, his decision does not remove from your shoulders the onus of comforting and fostering the girl. Considering you have never met Mr. Adams, and, as I understand it, Mr. Pinkney has met him only once, it would be quite improper for you to ignore his instructions and take matters into your own hands.

I am sorry, very sorry and disappointed that this development will remove all possibility of your coming to Highbury for Christmas. But, quite aside from Sophy, after your report of Mr. Pinkney's feelings in the matter as far as travelling with little Edward was concerned, I had not much hope. I was only tantalizing you a little with talk of plum puddings in case you might be tempted.

Our ball is on Saturday, and all Highbury is agog, or, in the case of the girls in this school, a-twitter. I understand William Pringle has invited some young men—Cambridge friends—down for the occasion. To provide these young gallants with partners, Mrs. Pringle has sent an invitation to any of my young ladies who are fifteen years of age and older, which

119

is good of her. But, oh, the anguish and mortification of those who are denied by a few weeks or months this incomparable benefaction. I shall be glad when the ball is over, because the commotion and the preoccupation with dress is such as to render any attempt at instruction fruitless. Miss Richardson was lamenting only this morning that it is quite impossible to persuade the girls to take the least interest in either the Roman emperors or the map of France. They are very happy, however, to practise their dancing and their curtseys!

Now that the famous hounds have arrived and are settled into their new homes, Mr. William Pringle seems to be more at leisure. Louisa and Lavinia report having met him by chance several times in the village. Sometimes Mr. Rutherford is of the party, and the four of them have walked about together and visited the various houses where the hounds are lodged. Each animal has a name, apparently. All this is very foreign to what one is used to. Louisa is now collecting quotations on Hunting. I have told her to look up Artemis and Diana.

As I believe I mentioned, I had seen to it that the Abbey Mill Farm party should be invited to the ball. I did not know quite how they would contrive, having no carriage. It was not in my power to offer hospitality to Robert Martin and Harriet, but I did ask Elizabeth Martin if she would like to come here to dine and dress and spend the night. She could have shared a bed with one of the twins, or they could have shared, and she could have had one to herself. But I was delighted to learn that the Martin family have been offered the Donwell carriage for the evening. This bespeaks such goodwill on the part of Emma and Mr. Knightley as gives me the greatest satisfaction.

I shall write again on Sunday and tell you all.

Yours aff:ly,
M. Goddard

Letter 46

(From Mrs. Pinkney to Mrs. Goddard)

Hans Place
Saturday 30 November 1816

My dear Mary,

It is Saturday evening, and I am thinking of you and your ball. You must even at this moment be arraying yourself in your black satin dress and putting on the locket with our father's hair. Your girls and your balls and your social goings-on in Highbury seem another world from the sober business of life in London. Here there is forever some contingency or other to contend with—largely associated with Sophy. But tonight I am light-hearted.

I have bought my muslin and the dressmaker is hard at work upon my new gown. It is to be trimmed with white satin ribbon rosettes and glass bugle beads. I am sure it will be most elegant. Mr. Pinkney remarks that it is quite amazing the degree of pleasure a female appears to derive from the prospect of a new gown. I try to explain to him that there is more to it than the mere gown, itself. It has something to do with being a woman, a desire to have other people regard one with approval. He asks if I suppose that a stranger seeing me for the first time would discern any difference between my wearing a new gown or an old one. I tell him that a new gown gives a woman a presence, a radiance, an *éclat.* Because she knows she is looking her best she is affable and amiable, which indeed can be observed by everyone. This would not be the case, I assure him, if she were feeling inferior and dejected for being seen *yet again* in the same old dress. He laughed and said he did not think an intelligent woman could talk such nonsense, but he was glad if I was happy. Yes, I told him, I am very happy and I went on to describe how, in my mind's eye, I pictured us ascending the stairs at the *soirée*, and hearing our name called out by a powdered footman and everyone turning to stare. And why should they be staring? Because they are admiring my gown, of course. He said how could I harbour such fantasies, and how differently women think from men. It was not at all how he viewed the prospect of the evening. Well, dear Mary, it will be a treat for us to go out alone together. No Sophy. No Captain Gordon. I am much looking forward to it.

Another reason I am cheerful is because tomorrow for the first time in many weeks we shall have the pleasure of dining alone together in our own house. To celebrate, I have ordered a particularly good dinner—oysters and a stuffed turbot followed by orange pudding. Sophy sent a note round this morning, she will not be coming tomorrow. Something is going on at the school, apparently. I am glad, for her sake, that she is at last included in whatever the circumstance is, and glad for ours that we can for once be without her.

Our other most regular guest will also be absent. Captain Gordon is dining with some old cronies he has met up with through his new connexions at the Admiralty. I am happy to report that his pension has come through at last. It is gratifying to see him looking so cheerful and with his head held high. A little money, and he has become a different person: is there a moral in this, Mary? I think there must be. Monday morning he leaves us to return to Portsmouth. This happy outcome is the direct result of the dinner-party. I met Isabella in the park today and told her how grateful I was and that I trusted this made her feel the little ruse she had had to employ was worthwhile.

I am greatly rejoiced, not only for Captain Gordon's sake, but also for our own. I love society, as you know dear Mary, but it does not suit my temperament to be the gracious hostess with such unremitting regularity. With no end in sight, I am in danger of becoming a very *ungracious* one.

Yours affectionately,
Charlotte

Letter 47

(From Mrs. Suckling to Mrs. Elton)

Maple Grove
nr. Bristol
1 December 1816

You cannot possibly be more disappointed than I am, my dear Augusta. It is too, too long that I have been confined to Bristol. I was vastly looking forward to London. I had high expectations of our shopping expeditions and parties of pleasure in the barouche-landau. Oh, that accursed equipage! The expense of having it repaired by some wretched thieving villain, knowing we were quite at his mercy, was immense. Mr. Suckling is still very displeased with James. He feels that if he were paying proper attention he would have seen the hole in the road and avoided it.

Sir Percy Lushley is known by name to Mr. Suckling, who was vastly disappointed at not being able to meet him as you had arranged.

So many things, it seems, conspire to vex us. The wall of my kitchen garden is still not finished. Following a trifling disagreement over the number of days worked, the man I had building it just walked off without a word. Would you not think he would be glad to be employed? I cannot understand that class

123

of person. They have nothing, and they make no effort to acquire anything. The idea of putting in an honest day's work is quite anathema to them. Very provoking, indeed. At this rate the wall will not be done before the frost sets in.

Pray excuse me. I am in an ill-humour and not disposed to write more.

Yours,
Selina Suckling

Letter 48

(From Mrs. Goddard to Mrs. Pinkney)

Hartfield
Sunday

It is three o'clock in the morning, my dear Charlotte. Our ball is over, and I regret to tell you that although it began in fine style, it very nearly ended in tragedy. I am at this moment sitting by Louisa's bed at Hartfield, too wrought-up to sleep. To relieve my feelings and give me an occupation *and* to keep me from falling asleep while I sit here, I will relate the circumstances.

To begin at the beginning: yesterday, how strange it is to write that word, I may as well write *last year*, it seems so long since *yesterday*, the day of the great event, a month exactly since the Pringles arrived in Highbury. Well, *yesterday*, I deemed it best to cancel morning lessons. The girls were far too excited for it to be of the smallest use to attempt any instruction, besides, I thought Miss Nash, Miss Price and Miss Richardson also deserved a little free time to get ready. Thus the extra hours were happily spent in titivation and curling hair, with much running back and forth between bedrooms borrowing and exchanging ribbons and stockings and necklaces and fans.

124

Mrs. Pringle had most kindly offered her carriage. Although the distance is not great between Hartfield and the school, she was concerned that my young ladies should be walking in the night air at this time of year. So it was arranged that her coachman was to make several excursions back and forth between the two houses until everyone had been transported. This was a not inconsiderable number. Besides the twins and me, there were also the nine young ladies of more than fifteen years of age as well as the three teachers. (Now you are not to be comparing me to Madame Dubois, my dear Charlotte. Those girls left behind were very adequately supervised by Sarah and Alice, as well as the maids, with instructions that John was to come for me immediately if I were needed.)

That I should arrive early was an especial request from Mrs. Pringle. For moral support, she said. The carriage called for us at a quarter to eight and within a matter of minutes Louisa, Lavinia and I were conveyed to the door of Hartfield. Even as we were ringing the bell the horses were turning around in the gravel sweep preparing for the return journey to the school. Memories of former days quite overcame me as we stood waiting to be admitted. I recalled how often over the years Mrs. and Miss Bates and I had been set down by James at this very spot and had happily entered to play cards with Mr. Woodhouse.

But when Greenwood, the Pringle butler, opened the door and we walked into the once-familiar rooms and beheld them blazing with light and alive with voices, to say nothing of the sound of a violin and a piano tuning, all such nostalgic recollections vanished. It is a very different Hartfield now.

We had rid ourselves of our cloaks and pelisses in the vestibule. Mrs. Pringle was passing through the hall and immediately came forward and welcomed us most warmly. Through the open drawing-room door I could see Mr. Rutherford—who presumably must have been invited even earlier than ourselves—and Mr. Pringle talking to five or six young men. Mr. Pringle immediately left his friends to pay his respects to us, and I observed him gazing with undisguised satisfaction at Louisa

125

and Lavinia. They, I must say, did look exceedingly pretty in their white muslin dresses, trimmed with pink roses, and wearing around their necks the pink coral bead necklaces, sent by their parents from India. Although their eyes were sparkling with delight, I perceived, however, that they were more than a little over-awed by this great occasion so long awaited. I believe they were quite struck when they realized that the William Pringle they had so light-heartedly teased when they had met him for the first time, was actually one of a coterie of fashionable young Cambridge men, all standing there together, tall, animated and at ease, quite lords of creation in fact.

Mr. Pringle led the girls into the drawing-room and introduced them to his friends. Meanwhile, in that promising period of calm which always precedes a party, when everything is anticipated but the guests have not yet arrived, Mrs. Pringle proposed showing me the arrangements she had made for the evening. While the young people were becoming acquainted, we strolled together through the rooms and I duly admired the dining-room, laid for supper with several long tables, the library, set out for cards with fresh packs and plenty of candles, and the drawing-room arranged for dancing. The furniture had been pushed back against the walls, and the carpets taken away except for the hearth rug in front of a splendid fire. It was around this fire that Louisa and Lavinia and the young men were gathered. I was pleased to note that the girls were already losing their initial bashfulness, and, encouraged by the attentions of the young men, were beginning to sparkle with all their accustomed vivacity.

Then the doorbell rang, and sounds of the first guests arriving were heard. I was preparing to sit down quietly in a corner and watch the developing scene when Mrs. Pringle summoned me.

"Mrs. Goddard," said she, "would you be so good as to come and stand in the hall and help to receive the guests?"

I must have looked somewhat taken aback, because she continued, "If you would be so obliging, I should deem it a great favour. I believe our neighbours will feel more at ease if they recognize a familiar face, and you can whisper to William and me the particulars of each family as they arrive. Come, William, we should take up our position," and she led the way into the hall and stood at the foot of the staircase.

I observed young Mr. Pringle cast a wistful eye at the group round the fire as he rather reluctantly followed his mother, though he did question whether it was really necessary for him to stand there, since she had Mrs. Goddard already with her.

"William, my dear, you cannot be serious? You would not want *not* to meet our new neighbours, at least those who arrive before the music begins. When the dancing commences you must certainly open the ball. Have you engaged your partner, yet?"

Mr. Pringle said that, yes, indeed, he had asked one of the Miss Ludgroves, and had told Mr. Rutherford he should ask the other.

"Is Charles not allowed to choose his own partner, then?" said she with a good-humoured smile.

"Of course he may. Only if I did not give him a prod, who knows how long he might be about it."

His mother laughed, and said something to me about Mr. Rutherford being so excessively retiring. We three had just arranged ourselves, when the door from the entrance vestibule opened and Greenwood began to call out names as the guests entered in a steady stream.

Among the vanguard was the first of the three contingents from my school. I heard my pupils chattering and giggling in the entrance and Miss Nash trying to quiet them. Like Louisa and Lavinia, on seeing the company, they became suddenly quite abashed, but they curtseyed to Mrs. Pringle very prettily, however. It was something we had been assiduously practising ever since the invitation arrived: how to enter a room, and curtsey to the hostess. Miss Nash is particularly graceful and elegant in this respect—she was once in London society, before her father lost his money—and it was she who instructed them. Having paid their respects, they moved into the drawing-room where the young men were still standing. Bees to a honey pot, followed by Miss Nash. I overheard Mr. Rutherford asking her shyly for their names, and they were properly and ceremoniously introduced to the Cambridge men. One is glad when things are done right. There is a satisfaction in it.

Next to arrive were Mr. and Mrs. Weston. The Westons are such a pleasant, chatty, good-natured couple that they are general favourites with everyone and are welcome everywhere. I do not know what Mrs. Weston's feelings may have been on entering the house which she had called home for seventeen years. She must have found it markedly changed—in atmosphere, at least, even if most of the furniture is the same. After they had greeted Mrs. Pringle, whom they had previously met at church, and made room for others who were behind them, I saw Mrs. Weston looking about her with great interest, and thought that doubtless tomorrow she will regale Emma with every detail.

The Coles came next. To my surprise they brought three of my girls from the school with them. Apparently it had suddenly struck Mrs. Cole as they were passing that their little daughters had told them of the invitation to the fifteen-year-olds. She made Mr. Cole stop the carriage. She was so ashamed of herself, she said, that she had not thought of it before. She offered to convey two of the girls, or three, if they did not mind being crowded. She had absolutely, as she told me, to convince Miss Richardson of the propriety of their accepting the offer, but since the girls were so eager, and it meant one less journey for the Pringle's coachman, Miss Richardson had been persuaded.

Very soon afterwards the whole of Highbury—what you call the ragtag and bobtail, my dear Charlotte—came flocking in. Although the butler was calling out their names, at Mrs. Pringle's request as they approached, I whispered in her ear such remarks as, "Mrs. Stokes of the Crown." "Mr. Cox and his family. He is our lawyer in Highbury." "Here is the Martin family. Robert Martin is tenant of the Abbey Mill Farm at Donwell.

His wife and his sister were both pupils at my school."

I believe the Martins made a most favourable impression. Robert Martin is not a handsome man. But he looks good-humoured and pleasant. Harriet is still a beautiful young woman, and Elizabeth Martin's whole sterling character shines in her face and manner. I was very pleased indeed to see Mrs. Martin again. Our friendship, which suffered a slight coolness at one time caused by Harriet's original refusal of her valuable son, is now quite restored. I felt that she and Mrs. Pringle might enjoy each other's acquaintance, both being sensible, unpretentious women, and I tried to encourage a conversation between them.

Since no one else was arriving at that particular moment, they did indeed begin to talk, mentioning the countryside around Highbury, and how little of it, heretofore, Mrs. Pringle had seen. But she was planning some excursions in the carriage if the weather remained fine. I was listening to them with half an ear while I made conversation with William, but before long, to my surprise and pleasure, I overheard Mrs. Martin inviting Mrs. Pringle to call on her at her cottage, and Mrs. Pringle promising to do so. I did not think Mrs. Pringle's very superior wealth would be an impediment to intimacy on *her* side, though I thought it might be a small hindrance on Mrs. Martin's. But Mrs. Pringle is so friendly, so unassuming, that in spite of her affluence she makes people with far fewer worldly goods feel quite at ease with her.

Sufficient numbers were now present to enable the dancing to begin. A preliminary chord was struck on the piano, the violinist drew his bow across his strings. The buzz of conversation faded to a murmur as those girls who were already engaged looked with arch expectation towards their partners, and those who were not shot pleading or timid glances in the direction of the young men. Oh, my dear Charlotte, the agony of a ball. I would not be seventeen again for all the tea in China.

William Pringle, who had been fidgeting from one foot to the other in excited impatience, was now dismissed by his mother with an indulgent smile.

"William, do go and begin. Any tardy arrivals will have to make your acquaintance later."

In fact nearly all the guests had arrived. Very prompt they were in their impatience to see Hartfield and their curiosity to discover how their neighbours would conduct themselves on the occasion.

Mr. Pringle and Mr. Rutherford and the twins took their places at the top of the set. To them was to be the honour of opening the ball. Oh, those two girls! They positively shone with happiness and excitement. All their former diffidence had vanished under the confiding attentions of the young men. They were the handsomest girls in the room, and they knew it. But I alone, I imagine, understood what each was thinking as she took her position in the set: *I am actually going to dance with A Man!* For at school, you know, and in dancing class, they can practise only with each other. Elizabeth Martin, I was pleased to note, was standing up with young Cox.

As the sets were forming and the music was about to begin, I saw Mr. Weston say something in a low voice to Mrs. Weston and her give a nod of approval. He then approached Mrs. Pringle and invited her to dance, which I thought was very proper of him. But she declined, said she preferred to enjoy the young people's performance. Mr. Weston then looked in my direction and smiled, but I smiled back and shook my head. Having done his duty he was able to lead Mrs. Weston to the set. I have not seen them perform together before. If the dance is an emblem of marriage, then I should say they shewed themselves most perfectly matched.

The first pair of dances was just over when Mr. and Mrs. Perry came bustling in, full of apologies for being late. There had been some emergency at Clayton Park which Mr. Perry had had to attend. What a life an apothecary leads, my dear Charlotte. Never any cessation of care for the health of others. I do not know what we would have done this evening without Mr. Perry—but I am getting ahead of myself.

I had just reached thus far, when Louisa stirred and moaned

130

in her bed. I got up and sponged her face with cool water. Luckily, she still sleeps. Meantime, writing this account—talking to you—helps ease my mind of its burden.

M.G.

Letter 48 (cont.)

One of the maids, who has stayed up to be of assistance, brought me a cup of tea. Having drunk it, and feeling somewhat refreshed, I shall continue my account of the ball. At first, the ordinary folk of Highbury were too much overcome by the splendour of their surroundings to do much more than huddle together and gaze about them nervously. But Mrs. Pringle was so amiable and sympathetic, so hospitable and anxious for their welfare, so interested in asking them about themselves and so pressing with offers of wine and suggestions of dancing or cards, that it was not very long before they began to shed their fears and look about them with confidence: some few actually standing up and forming their own set.

As you may imagine, dear Charlotte, I watched all this with the greatest interest. Then Mrs. Perry and Mrs. Cole spoke of whist to their husbands. Mr. Cole begged to be excused. One did not often, in Highbury, said he, have the opportunity of watching pretty young ladies dancing. But Mr. Perry was willing, and so I was invited to make up the table. Like Mr. Cole, I would have much preferred watching the young people, but there being no fourth available at that moment I could not very well refuse. In the library we found several others already at play, among them Dr. and Mrs. Wilson and Mr. and Mrs. Cox.

I dutifully endured a rubber, and was puzzling how I could extricate myself from spending the entire evening at the table, when I recollected Miss Prince, who has a passion for cards and not many opportunities for indulging it. So at a convenient moment, I was able to offer my excuses and fetch her from the alcove where she was sitting with the other chaperones.

In the drawing room I found a chair beside Mrs. Martin. She remarked on the changes at Hartfield, now ringing with music and young laughter. Not that she, herself, had ever been inside the place before, but she vividly recalled that Harriet had often observed how quiet and dignified the house was in Mr. Woodhouse's time, when she was Emma's *protégée* and Hartfield had been almost a second home to her: never a raised voice or a hastily closed door broke the stillness. But, said Mrs. Martin, she must beg my pardon, of course I could corroborate her statements. I had been used to come here often, had I not, and was it not a great improvement now, so cheerful and hospitable? I said indeed many people would think so. I did not tell her that I felt sad for the loss of old friends and former days, and privately wondered if the ancestors on the walls might not be cringing in their frames. For a few moments we sat in silence watching the spirited spectacle before us. Then Mrs. Martin mentioned the kindness of Mr. Knightley in making his carriage available to them.

"So truly attentive of him. I really do not know how we might have contrived, otherwise," said she.

"Mr. Knightley is a very benevolent man," I observed. "It would have been a great pity if you had not been able to come to the ball. I am pleased to see Elizabeth is dancing with Mr. Rutherford."

"Yes," said Mrs. Martin, "but the last pair of dances she had to sit out. She was beside me without a partner when Mr. Rutherford came up and asked her. He seems a very pleasant young man. I often regret that Elizabeth is so cut off from young society at Donwell, especially now her sister is married. There is only Robert and Harriet for company of her own age."

At that moment Louisa and Lavinia swept by us, laughing and twirling round with abandon. I murmured something about youth and exuberance

"Those girls of yours," said she, "those Ludgrove twins are

remarkably pretty. The men quite flock about them."

"Ah," said I, "alas, there are always too many pretty girls and not enough men at a ball. I do not know why that should be. But it is quite an immutable law."

Mrs. Martin agreed, and said it had certainly been the case when she was young. I thought to myself how unjust it was that the likes of the Ludgrove twins will always find partners, and the likes of Elizabeth Martin very often will not.

I then felt the need to say something encouraging to Mrs. Martin, and I told her that in the course of twenty years hundreds of girls had passed through my hands, and it was not an exaggeration to declare that Elizabeth was one of the most delightful. She, also, in my opinion, had a most sterling character. Mrs. Martin said this was all very gratifying, but having a sterling character did not necessarily attract a husband. In fact, it very often had quite the opposite effect. Still, she, Mrs. Martin, would soon be getting to an age when it would be very pleasant to have a daughter always at home, and Elizabeth seemed perfectly content. I thought these sentiments a little premature, Charlotte. The girl is, after all, only twenty-one, even if no prospects have yet presented themselves. But to myself I commended Mrs. Martin for giving nothing away: hardly intimating by so much as the smallest hint that she wished Elizabeth, or Elizabeth wished herself, married.

Meanwhile, all my pretty, fifteen-year-old young ladies—their bashfulness entirely forgotten in the flutter of the flattering attentions they were receiving—were almost beyond themselves in silliness. Come Monday morning, I reflected, it will not be easy to repeat the dates of the accession of the kings of England. The good folk of Highbury, also, had completely shed their reserve and were cavorting with enthusiasm. Miraculous to behold, Mr. Perry had forsaken the whist table and was actually dancing with Miss Nash.

It was soon time for supper. The musicians retired to the servants' hall for a well-earned rest, and everybody else trooped into the dining-room. For some reason this put me in mind of

Miss Bates. And I recalled the Westons' ball and the supper at the Crown and how she had been concerned that Jane should wear her tippet and not catch cold. Good soul! Always thinking of others, but who, now, I wondered, thinks of her? I felt very sorry that she should not be here on this occasion, which she would have so much enjoyed.

Mrs. Martin and I walked together into the dining-room and found the twins already sitting down. They were in a cluster at the end of a long table chatting away with Mr. Rutherford and Mr. Pringle and Robert Martin and Harriet and Elizabeth. Both Elizabeth and Harriet were at school with the Ludgrove girls. Although there is three or four years' difference in age, Harriet and the twins, in particular, have much in common, having all been parlour boarders. Later, I was pleased to note Robert Martin, Elizabeth and Mr. Rutherford talking more seriously with their heads close together. Mr. Rutherford could learn much from Robert Martin in many respects. At the other end of the table, making a vast deal of noise with the young men from Cambridge, were my fifteen-year-olds. I thought my presence might have a sobering effect, but nothing of the kind. As the saying goes, they had got the bit between their teeth and were running with it. Mrs. Martin and I joined Mrs. Pringle, who was sitting among the more sober, middle-aged people in another part of the room. They seemed to be having difficulty hearing each other speak. I saw that they were half-amused, half-exasperated by the shrieks of the young people. Miss Nash asked Mrs. Pringle if she should stop them, and Mrs. Pringle said, not at all, she was pleased to see everyone so happy.

Undoubtedly it was proving to be a most successful ball. As soon as supper was over the young people were eager to be dancing again, and there was a general movement back to the drawing-room. I heard Louisa say, "You must listen to our duet. Lavinia and me's been practising prodigiously." Of course they were pressed by their friends to perform before the musicians reappeared. They drew up the piano bench and sat down. That Mozart duet! I believe I could almost play it myself, I have heard them practise it so often. Of course they were a charming sight, the two of them, so young, so handsome, and so alike. They played with a great deal of spirit—if not too accurately—and it was plain that all the young men were completely bewitched. Then the real musicians appeared, wiping their mouths and ready to take over the instrument once more.

Earlier in the evening, before supper, someone had stepped behind a curtain and opened a window (whatever would Mr. Woodhouse have said?) and the room had chilled off considerably. Mrs. Pringle was quite concerned that the girls might catch cold, and called for the butler to make up the fire.

"Oh, I can manage that, m'am," said Mr. Pringle. "Do not trouble Greenwood. He has enough to do." And he snatched up some firewood that was lying by the hearth and threw it on the dying embers, then seizing the bellows and working them vigorously very shortly had a roaring blaze going up the chimney. "There," said he, "that will soon warm up the room again."

The musicians were preparing to play. William Pringle and Louisa had established themselves as first couple. They called out to Mr. Rutherford to bring Lavinia and join them. At that moment, while they were standing on the hearth rug, a spark flew out of the fire and narrowly missed falling on one of the girls' skirts. Mr. Pringle promptly stamped it out with his foot, in the process nearly stepping on Elizabeth Martin, who, lacking a partner, was sitting on a chair nearby.

"Do be careful," cried Mrs. Pringle. "That is too big a fire, William. You should have let Greenwood do it."

Her son paid no heed. The young people were ready. Two sets were forming; the musicians beginning a lively Scottish reel.

"Hey ho," he cried. "My favourite. Come, Charles, let us see how fast we can spin our partners." And although it was after one o'clock, and the chaperones were drooping in their chairs, the young people seemed to be tireless, swinging each other around—you know the figure, Charlotte, four hands across, much vigorous whirling about and sudden changing of direction.

Mr. Pringle and Louisa were gyrating the most furiously. Good heavens, I thought, at such a speed I should think she would be dizzy. I was a little distance away watching, when suddenly! Louisa's foot caught in the hearth rug and she crashed to the floor, the skirt of her gown fell into the fire, and in a flash she was in a sheet of flame. The screams! The horror of it! Everybody was paralyzed by shock hardly able to comprehend the danger. But not Elizabeth. While the others stood frozen, immobile, she leapt to her feet, and regardless of her own safely, seized the hearth rug and with the flames flaring all about her rolled it round and round Louisa. As soon as Mr. Rutherford realized what she was about, he rushed forward to help, tearing off his coat and employing it to stifle the flames.

As abruptly as it happened, it was over. Of course I ran to Louisa, and Mr. Perry, summoned from the card room, came running also, calling for everyone to stand back, for Greenwood to fetch a glass of water, and for his wife to bring his bag, which he happened to have brought with him from Clayton Park (much to Mrs. Perry's chagrin, as I later heard). Louisa was now screaming in agony. A most terrible sound, Charlotte, I never hope to hear the like again. The rug was unrolled. She lay on the floor, writhing in pain, her gown charred and stuck to her skin, her pretty face screwed up in suffering. Mr. Perry put some laudanum drops in a glass of water, and raising Louisa's head insisted she drink it, telling her it would ease the pain. He declared she must be carried to a bed, and asked for cloths to be brought soaked in tea. Lavinia was weeping in sympathy for her sister, and poor William Pringle was ashen with shock. A burly impassive footman carried Louisa, moaning, upstairs, while Mr. Perry and I and Mrs. Pringle, William Pringle and Lavinia, all in various states of distress, followed behind. On Mr. Perry's instructions, a maid flew about and prepared a bed with a waterproof sheet. He asked that I stay to assist him, and dismissed everyone else. It was some time before the laudanum took effect. I held Louisa's hand and talked to her as soothingly as my own agitation would allow. Eventually she lapsed into semi-consciousness. Mr. Perry then poured cold water over her scorched gown. I tell you, Charlotte, it was a pitiful sight. The poor girl cried out as we ever so gently pulled away the blackened material. Her left leg was the most affected. A horrible sight, which quite sickened me and which I will not describe. Mr. Perry laid the cloths that had been soaked in tea very carefully across the burns.

Mrs. Pringle, deeply concerned, was hovering outside the door. Seeing her, Mr. Perry asked if she had a whalebone corset handy. Stifling her surprise at such a question, she obediently went and fetched one. Mr. Perry then so arranged it over the burned limb that the bedclothes would not press upon it. He gave instructions that Louisa must not be moved, must remain there as quietly as possible. It was now well past two o'clock in the morning. There was nothing more he could do for the present, he said, but when she woke up, she must be given more laudanum, and he left me the bottle, and directions, and promised to return after breakfast.

Mr. William Pringle and Mr. Rutherford then reappeared at the door with whispered anxious inquiries. I told them Mr. Perry had said Louisa would be all right, that she would recover, although she would be in pretty severe pain for several days. If it were not for the prompt action of Elizabeth Martin, I remarked, there was no question that she would now be dead.

"Where is Miss Martin?" asked Mr. Rutherford.

William Pringle replied that he supposed she had gone home as all the other guests had done, including Lavinia, who, incidentally, had had to be almost forcibly dragged away by Miss Nash. The only people left were those who were actually staying in the house. Mr. Rutherford remarked what a pity it was that in the anxiety of the moment nobody had even commented to Elizabeth on her action.

"That is like Elizabeth," I replied. "She would go home. She would not wait for thanks or praise. She is that sort of young woman."

"I am sure she is," remarked Mr. Rutherford. "That is the impression I formed of her. I hope she was not burned also. I do not know how she could have escaped."

"We shall find out tomorrow," I said.

"Tomorrow is now today," said William Pringle.

This, my dear Charlotte, was the conclusion of the ball. And here I now sit beside the mercifully sleeping Louisa. Good Mrs. Pringle who is extremely distressed by this accident, has been most concerned that I should not be overtired, and has offered one of the maids to sit here in my stead. But I declined. If Louisa should wake up, I could not bear that she should find a stranger beside her. In that case, said Mrs. Pringle, she herself would sit there. But I assured her that it was my choice and that there was nothing to be gained by her going without rest, and on condition that I promised to ring the bell if I needed anything, she was persuaded to go to bed.

There we are, my dear Charlotte. It has distracted me to write to you. But now, since I have a comfortable wing chair, and a footstool and since Louisa seems to be sleeping soundly—thank heavens for the laudanum, an apothecary should always take his bag to a ball—perhaps I shall try and have a little nap, myself.

Yours aff:ly,
Mary

Letter 49

(From Mrs. Goddard to Mrs. Pringle)

Monday evening

My dear Madam,

Thank you for your kind note of inquiry received an hour ago. I apologise for not replying at once by your footman, but Mr. Perry was here seeing to the patient, and I was not at liberty.

I have to thank you for the use of your carriage this morning. We had as comfortable a short journey hither as was possible under the circumstances. When we arrived home, John carried her upstairs to bed.

Mr. Perry is very sanguine. He assures me there will be no visible disfigurement. At the moment Louisa is still in considerable pain, but on Mr. Perry's direction I have been giving her laudanum drops at regular intervals, and she has been asleep most of the day. When she was awake I was able to persuade her to drink a little nourishing chicken broth, which Sarah made especially for her.

I hope, my dear Mrs. Pringle, that you are not too distressed by this misadventure. Young people will be exuberant and careless of danger. It is part of their charm. One would not wish them to be as sober and cautious as we are. We can only be grateful that the consequence of this accident is not a lasting tragedy.

I beg that you will think only of the great pleasure you gave to the people of Highbury. I assure you that the agreeable evening they spent at Hartfield will be an occasion they will remember long after Louisa's unfortunate accident has faded into a distant memory. I trust young Mr. Pringle will also put this behind him. It was something which in the whole course of his life he may never see happen again. Thanks to Elizabeth Martin there will be no serious outcome.

Yours, etc.
M. Goddard

P.S. I had a note from Mrs. Martin this morning. Elizabeth's hands were indeed quite badly burned by the flames, and she is in some pain, but by the application of lard they have been soothed. She would not allow her mother to call Mr. Perry.

Letter 50

(Captain Gordon to Charlotte Marlowe)

Hans Place
Monday 2 December 1816

My dear Lottie,

I fear I shall not be returning today as I had hoped.

A tragedy has struck this family. Mr. Pinkney's niece has run away from that abominable seminary. Mr. and Mrs. Pinkney are distraught, apprehensive for the child herself as well as deeply concerned for the anguish this will cause her father.

In consideration of all the kindness I have been shewn, and the trouble Mrs. Pinkney has gone to on my behalf, I feel I must stay on to be of what assistance I can. Mr. Pinkney is not a practical man, and has taken this turn of events very hard.

Ever your most affectionate father,
A. J. Gordon

140

Letter 51

(From Mrs. Pinkney to Mrs. Goddard)

Hans Place
Tuesday 3 December 1816

I hardly know whether to address this to the school or to Hartfield, but I trust it will reach you quickly wherever you are.

Disaster for us as well as for you.

How could I have been so gullible! I actually believed that Sophy had some other engagement when she said she could not come to dinner on Sunday, and was so glad for her sake that presumably at last she had made friends with someone at the school.

A friend, indeed! She has run away with the footman. Madame Dubois sent a note round yesterday morning to say that both are missing. The sly girl, having told Madame she was with us, and told us she was at school, has had a whole day's head start. Quite clear *now* why she wanted five pounds.

And if they are discovered, declares Madame, wretched hypocrite that she is, we are not to expect her to have Sophy back at school again. Her unruly and perverse behaviour, says she, is a poor example to the other pupils. Such a parade of punctiliousness, from *that* woman of all people.

I am extremely provoked, Mary. Why should that obstinate and ungracious girl come intruding into our quiet, happy lives and cause us this distress? For years Mr. Pinkney heard nothing of Mr. Adams or his daughter, and now we are embroiled in anxiety and vexation. Of course Mr. P. feels responsible to his brother, though in my opinion it is not our fault in the least. What else could we have done except what we did do? Poor Mr. P. The circumstance has rekindled memories of his youth and his sister and what a sweet affectionate little girl she

141

was when he used to come home in the vacations from Oxford. Now he feels he has failed Sophia in not taking better care of her daughter and is overcome with conscience and regret. He looks worried half to death and yesterday evening retired to bed with an attack of gout, brought on, I am certain, by this deplorable event. Mr. Wingfield, who came to see him today, agrees with me this is entirely possible.

Oh, Mary, if only we had heeded your warning! *You* suspected she was up to no good. This would never have happened if we had sent Sophy to you instead of so scrupulously adhering to her father's wishes.

In spite of everything, my sympathies are very much with that unhappy man. What has he done to deserve such a blow? Is it revenge on her part for being sent to school in England? She might have spared his feelings, even if she did not consider ours. He doted on the girl. As you know, he has no other kith nor kin. His sole idea was that she should make an eligible match, and he could retire and live out his last years near her in England. Eligible? An Irish footman!

We hope she may be found before we need inform Mr. Adams. Mr. P. does not need to write to him as yet with the dread news, for luckily, as far as we are able to determine, there is no ship leaving for Barbadoes for about ten days. But if, *when*, Sophy is found, what in the world can Mr. P. say of the smallest comfort? I suppose the villain will have had his way with her, as the saying goes, and she will be ruined.

Captain Gordon has been immensely helpful. Although he was packed and ready to leave for Portsmouth, when the news came he immediately gave up his own plans and offered to go round to the seminary to interview Madame Dubois. You can imagine how grateful I was. I simply could not bring myself to set foot in that unbearable place and confront the unspeakable woman. So he went, and inquired on our behalf if anything is known of this footman, this Paddy O'Ryan. Madame treated him with scant civility, certainly no remorse, *she* was in no way to blame. She was almost sneering, he said, declaring that it was not her usual custom to accept such uncouth, colonial girls, and really she could not answer for Sophy's extraordinary action, nor had she the slightest idea where they might have gone. (Wretched, odious woman, sitting on a year's fees in advance!) Of course we hoped there might be a possibility of tracing their whereabouts through the man's relations. But as you might suppose, nothing whatever is known of Paddy O'Ryan, or whether he even has any family. As for Sophy, I cannot imagine what she hopes to gain by this manoeuvre. She is so immature, she probably looks no further ahead than the immediate phenomenon of her having successfully escaped from the hated school. But to what purpose? Thinking back to previous conversations with her, she does seem to have been bedazzled by the man. I gather he did not even have proper references, but was engaged on his appearance and charm solely. How sick I am of that charm. If I could get my hands on the wretch, I'd charm him all right!

We have been trying to determine where they might go. Captain Gordon, after he left Madame, kindly went on his own initiative to the Golden Cross to inquire there if a tall Irishman with a young girl had bought places on any of the coaches leaving town. It was a clever idea of his, but it came to nothing. Yet it seems unlikely they would remain in London, and as far as we know they have not funds to pay for lodgings for any length of time. On the remote possibility that the man may marry her in order to extort money from her father, Captain Gordon left yesterday evening for Gretna Green in search of them. Such an expedition would be quite beyond Mr. Pinkney. He was glad to give him the money to travel by post as rapidly as possible. It is exceedingly good of Captain Gordon, for it is 309 miles to Gretna from London and at this time of year will not be an easy journey. He expected to be at least three nights on the road, so we must wait in suspense. Suspense? But what makes one imagine such a person as an Irish footman will trouble to marry the girl? And does one *want* such a marriage? I imagine after he has had his pleasure he will abandon her. He is bound to be utterly unscrupulous. He seems to have led a rackety, unsettled sort of life. I am so sorry for Mr. Adams. Such is the dismal outcome of his plans to make an elegant lady out of his daughter.

I beg your pardon to be full of gloom, dear Mary, when you, yourself, must be so anxious and still recovering from the shock of such a narrowly averted tragedy. What a mercy Elizabeth Martin was so quick-witted. I hope Louisa goes on well. Selfishly, I am too full of our own catastrophe to comment further at the moment.

Your extremely provoked sister,
Charlotte

Letter 52

(From Mrs. Goddard to Mrs. Pinkney)

Highbury
Wednesday 4 December 1816

Yours has just come, my dear Charlotte. I am sitting down at once to send you all my sympathy and tender thoughts in your distress. Yet, I do beg that you and Mr. Pinkney will not reproach yourselves unduly, and be quite overpowered with regret. You acted from the best of motives in following Sophy's father's wishes. You could not do *more*, given the circumstance of him adamantly refusing to take your advice. *That* must be your consolation—poor comfort though it may be.

I conjecture Sophy cannot vanish into the blue entirely. Somehow or other, even if it is not as soon as you would wish, eventually you are bound to hear of her. At least she is likely to write to her father if she is as attached to him as you say. As for her being "ruined," let us hope that it will not be so. Unlikely, I realize. But is it possible the man has some good feelings? Dear

Charlotte, I wish there was something I could do to help you. Please give my condolences to Mr. Pinkney. It is most unfortunate that this anxiety has made him ill again, when he has been free of gout for so long. I pray that you will not fret unduly and make yourself ill too.

It is well-known that girls can be very contrary in the years between childhood and marriage. I have often thought that is why my school is popular. Parents are happy to send their daughters off to be out of the way and let them acquire what education they can. But in Sophy's case it was too late and badly done. This fiasco has been the consequence.

I know you will want to hear about Louisa. She spent two nights at Hartfield. Unfortunately my duties at school did not permit me to be with her constantly, though her sister was with her when I was not and Mrs. Pringle was very kind. But on Monday morning she begged she might come home, where I could be always at hand to nurse her. Mr. Perry gave his permission and dosed her well with that blessed laudanum. William Pringle carried her down very carefully to the carriage and thus she was conveyed hither. She is happier, I think, in familiar surroundings and in having her sister with her. Mr. Perry comes every day, and Mrs. Pringle and William Pringle have been to call, but she has not yet felt equal to seeing them. The poor young man is very subdued and solicitous. I believe he feels very much to blame. I am sorry for him. At present she is in bed, but tomorrow or the next day I hope she will feel like lying upon the sopha. Elizabeth Martin came and brought her some oranges, but was considerate enough to stay only a few minutes.

But I will not prattle on about Highbury—I am sure your mind is on one subject only.

You know I am thinking of you constantly, please inform me as soon as you hear anything.

With best love,
Mary Goddard

Letter 53

Mrs. Smith's Lodgings
Portsmouth
Wednesday 4 December 1816

My dear Mrs. Pinkney,

I am so dreadfully distressed to hear that your niece has run away.

Let me say that if anyone can find her, I am sure my father can. He is very acute and resourceful. He is also very glad to be able to be of assistance to you and Mr. Pinkney after all you have done for him.

Terrible as it is, one does have to admire Sophy's spirit. Myself, I never had such courage. Often as I contemplated my escape from that place, I never could bring myself to open the door and walk out alone into the London streets. I imagined that if I did, I would end up in some dreadful House or other like poor Clarissa in Richardson's story.

Perhaps, then, it is not so bad that Sophy has a man with her. At least one hopes he will protect her from anything of that sort.

I will not take up more of your time, though you can be sure I am thinking of you very much.

Your sympathetic friend,
Charlotte Marlowe

P.S. Pray do not think of replying.

Letter 54

(From Mrs. Pinkney to Mrs. Goddard)

Hans Place
London
Thursday 5 December 1816

Yes, please, dear Mary, do prattle on, as you call it. You cannot think how much I long to be distracted from our present misery. I am counting the days until it is possible to hear from Captain Gordon. By my calculations, he should arrive in Gretna today. But we cannot depend on it, he did not leave until late in the afternoon on Monday. Even though he will send by express, I believe we must allow two more days before we can hope for any news.

It is all very well for you to make soothing remarks. But I blame myself. You warned us. I should have seen what was so obviously coming. I did not think I was so unperceptive. Perhaps, on reflection, it was not so much lack of perception as a desire to avoid trouble, not to have to take some decisive step or other—such as interview Madame Dubois, demand that the footman be dismissed and precipitate unpleasantness between Sophy and ourselves and ultimately her father. Unpleasantness of a very different order, my dear Mary, from your apple pie beds. Yet, I wonder, was it so obvious? Girls I have known do not do that sort of thing. Has anyone ever run away from *your* school?

Do write me a nice cheerful letter and tell me about your young people. I hope Louisa continues to improve. Are your matchmaking efforts likely to be successful?

Yours with love,
Charlotte

Letter 55

Highbury
6 December 1816

No, nobody has ever run away from my school, but then mine is a very different establishment from that of Madame Dubois. I suppose rather like a mother and her children, I am constantly aware of the state of mind and well-being of each of my girls. It would not be possible in a well-regulated family for one member to be unhappy and an affectionate mother not to know it. If I, or any of my three teachers, notice any girl looking at all cast down, we do our utmost to discover what is troubling her and to remedy it. But I do not wish to be appearing to give myself undue credit. To run away from Highbury would not be very easy. A young woman walking off alone through the country lanes would soon attract attention. It is far simpler to disappear into the streets of London. Out of the door and gone, if one so wished, and that is that. Well, my dear Charlotte, I depend upon you letting me know as soon as you hear from Captain Gordon.

Louisa is now able to be up and lying on the sopha. She is still in pain, but she begins to look happier and to talk about *when* she is recovered and will be able to do so and so. Her hair has had to be cut off where it was singed, then the other side of her head also to make it even. The short hair quite suits her, and it will soon grow again, I tell her, so she should not lament, but be grateful that she is alive and not permanently disfigured. There is no mistaking, now, one twin from the other.

Mrs. Pringle comes every day with her son to visit. The

division of the party falls naturally. I sit and talk on one side of the parlour with Mrs. Pringle—my head full of all that I should be doing, as you may imagine—while on the other side the young man perches beside Louisa's sopha and murmurs in her ear. Today, while half listening to Mrs. Pringle's account of her call on Mrs. Martin, I overheard him telling Louisa about his hounds. Owing to the ball and this accident, he and Mr. Rutherford have been out with some of the other men only once. Then I heard Louisa describing India, such as she remembers it. Lavinia sometimes joins us and participates in the conversation also, but being an active young woman, she does not care for sitting still so long, and has taken to going out with one of the other girls, Amelia Cooper, with whom she is friendly.

Yesterday these two walked as far as Donwell and back. Lavinia told me that they espied Mr. Rutherford fishing on the river bank, and thought they would go over and ask him if he had caught anything. Then they saw he already had company. Elizabeth Martin was sitting on a fallen tree beside him, and they were deep in conversation.

I hope she might not catch cold! To be sitting outside in December would certainly have incurred Mr. Woodhouse's disapprobation.

Yours aff:ly,

M. Goddard

P.S. I do not like to hear you talk of *matchmaking*, my dear Charlotte, it sounds so calculating. One can only put young people in the way of meeting each other—and perhaps smooth the way a little. But the rest must be left up to chance and to themselves.

Letter 56

(From Captain Gordon to Mr. Pinkney)

Gretna Green
Dumfriesshire
5 December 1816

My dear Sir,

I fear this letter will not bring you any joy. I arrived this morning, having travelled by day and by night in the hope of forestalling a wedding. I went directly to the smithy and made particular enquiries of the blacksmith there, who, as you know, performs all the marriages in Gretna. He assured me most positively that no one answering to the description of a tall Irishman with a young girl has been married by him in the past week.

I am sending this by express. I, myself, will follow immediately and hope to be with you within twenty-four hours of your receiving it. I have some other ideas and shall be happy on consultation with you both to pursue the search. I believe there is still hope of finding the young couple before the ship sails for Barbadoes and you must write and notify the father.

I am, dear sir,

Your most humble obdt. servt.
A. J. Gordon

Letter 57

(From Mrs. Pinkney to Mrs. Goddard)

Hans Place
7 December 1816

I send you the enclosed, dear Mary, which came by express late this evening. I hardly know whether it is good news or bad. At least she has not married the wretch, which would be eternal damnation.

It is excessively obliging of Captain Gordon to take this trouble on our behalf. I really do not know now what more he can do, or that we are justified in asking him to do. I am sure young Charlotte is disappointed her father is not returning home to Portsmouth as planned. Still, if when he comes, he insists on continuing the search I am sure we shall not prevent him.

I believe the Captain took quite a fancy to Sophy. He admired her originality and independence of spirit. He intimated he would be only too happy if he could find her and save her from what we perceive as a dreadful error. Mr. Pinkney is relieved that some action is being taken. The navy is so enterprising! He, himself, is absolutely unable to career about the countryside in post chaises making inquiries of blacksmiths, etc., even if he were not laid low with gout.

The evening party for Mr. Falconbridge is in a few days time. Neither of us feels like going—and at the moment Mr. Pinkney is definitely not able.

Yours aff.,
C. P.

P.S. I beg you will continue your letters about Highbury. Aside from the horrid accident to Louisa, your usually cheerful news quite takes both Mr. Pinkney's and my minds off our troubles. To hear that Mr. Rutherford and Elizabeth Martin have been seen together on the river bank is excessively agreeable. It reminds us that someone, somewhere, is happy and carefree. Something which we at present are not.

Letter 58

(From Mrs. Goddard to Mrs. Pinkney)

Highbury
8 December 1816

Home from church and I am replying to yours immediately, my dear Charlotte. I wish I knew what I could say of comfort. I am very sorry that Captain Gordon's quest to Gretna has been unsuccessful, and you therefore have this continuing worry, which I am sure is always uppermost in your mind.

For that reason I do most earnestly beg you to go to the party for Mr. Falconbridge. Your staying home will not make the smallest difference to Captain Gordon's success or failure in the recovery of Sophy, and it would be such a pity to deny yourself this much-anticipated pleasure. What about your new gown? Think how disappointed it will be not to be given an airing! Well, I am not often given to such flights of fancy, but I do believe the advice is good, so kindly heed it.

Louisa is very much better, you will be glad to hear. She says she is bored with the sopha, and has been walking very slowly about the school. Still in some discomfort, but her natural cheerfulness is beginning to assert itself.

It seems cruel and callous on my part to talk of happy things when you both are suffering, but since you have so instructed me, I shall proceed. The girls are getting more excited as each passing day brings the Christmas holidays nearer. I lament that you are not to be here—aside from Edward, I suppose your plans are dependent upon Sophy and she could yet turn up. But I will not press you, I realize you must abide by Mr. Pinkney's wishes. Meantime, I hear there are great preparations going forward at Donwell Abbey, readying the place for the invasion of the John Knightleys. Yes, my dear, it is indeed an invasion, seven children and their nursery maids. I understand that both the Knightley and the former Woodhouse carriage are to travel up to London to help transport them all to Highbury.

It has been some years since they had Christmas together at Donwell. Mr. Woodhouse's constitution had lately made it necessary that they should be always at Hartfield. According to Alice, Mrs. Hodges and Serle have been in their element, arranging it all and cooking and preparing. Is it not fortunate that these two women respect each other and work together so harmoniously? The Hartfield servants seem to have settled in well. I believe Mrs. Hodges is quite amazed at the change in her master since he has a wife to tease him into smiling and lively discourse instead of his spending the evenings alone at his accounts.

Now, remember my advice!

Yours aff:ly,
Mary

Letter 59

(From Sophy Adams to Mr. and Mrs. Pinkney)

My dear Uncle and Aunt:

I am afraid you will have been conserned.

This letter is to asure you I have come to no harm. I am perfeckly well and in safe hands.

Pray do not worry about me, nor try to find me. It would be trubbling yourself unnesessarily, and you would not be sucksessful.

I could endur that place, no more.

I will ask my father to repay you the £5.00 you lent me.

Your dutyfull neice,
Sophy Adams

P.S. I am sorry I did not write before. I had not pen or paper or oportuneity until today.

Letter 60

(From Mrs. Pinkney to Mrs. Goddard)

Hans Place
Sunday 8 December 1816

My dear Mary,

I wrote to you last night and now we have received this from Sophy this morning. I have made you a fair copy—having corrected the spelling! I am keeping the original to show to Captain Gordon, whom we expect hourly. The postmark is from a small post office on the Great West Road. It is stamped Friday 6 December, and must have been missent, for it took two days to reach us.

Of course we are greatly relieved. She is alive, at least. But what is one to make of it? Safe hands? What does that mean? *Where* she is, *what* she is doing, or intending to do, are complete mysteries. Why does she have *now* an opportunity of writing she did not have before? As you see she does not mention the Irishman, yet she must know that we would assume her to be with him. Is *he* the "safe hands?" Mr. P. says at least the girl has a conscience—she is aware that we would be worried half to death, and she is also honest enough to wish to repay the £5.00. In spite of myself, I cannot help think the better of her for it.

Later. I have been keeping this open, dear Mary, hoping Captain Gordon would come and I could give you more news. He returned from Gretna three hours ago. He would barely stop to change his linen and eat some cold meat, before he set off again with the letter in his pocket. He absolutely insisted, said he owed us so much, it was the least he could do, etc. etc. Yet I feel a little anxious. He is not young, and he has been travelling constantly day and night, this last week. It is quite astonishing the distances he has covered. Now, without stopping to rest, he is off again. He is certainly repaying tenfold any debt he might feel that he owed us. His perseverance is prodigious. A lesser man would not have the fortitude. He says he will go first to the post office from whence the letter was sent and make inquiries. The fact that it came from the Great West Road confirms his private theory as to where they may have gone. (Could it be Ireland?) He would not say more, however, because he did not want to raise expectations which might come to nothing. If he does not find them within the next few days we will be obliged to write to Sophy's father and tell him that his daughter has disappeared, we know not where.

Mr. Pinkney has been much encouraged since we heard

from Sophy. He feels more cheerful, though his gout is still bad. Mr. Wingfield comes every day and entreats him not to worry. He has seen more patients made ill by worry, he declares, than by any other cause.

Ever yours,
Charlotte

Letter 61

(*From Mrs. Goddard to Mrs. Pinkney*)

Highbury
9 December 1816

My dear Charlotte,

Our letters, both posted yesterday, have crossed.

I am so relieved for your sake that Sophy has written. At least the girl has some good feelings, some thought of what is owing to you and Mr. Pinkney. I agree, it makes one think more kindly of her that she considered you enough to write this letter and to make some sort of explanation. Evidently she intends to notify her father, if she has not already done so, since she talks of having him repay the money. I think this is the most encouraging aspect of the business. When you write to him, as I suppose you must now be obliged to do, you can mention this, which should be a consolation to him.

"Safe Hands?" Presumably this refers to the Irishman? That is a strange remark about not "troubling yourself unnecessarily," and that you would not be *successful* in finding her? She does not reckon, perhaps, on the acumen of the navy. Captain Gordon would be cognizant of places that a gentleman such as Mr. Pinkney, a scholar who has led a sheltered life, would be quite unaware of. Having received this first letter from the girl, my dear Charlotte, I am convinced you will hear again soon, one way or the other.

I hope Mr. Pinkney is becoming more resigned to what he cannot alter, and that you are not continuing to brood on the affair. You entertained Sophy, listened to her complaints and did what you could for her. Even gave her money. (With the best of intentions, of course!) I am sure with her determination, which you once spoke about, she would have run away whether she had money or no. Perhaps Mr. Adams will now realize he should have paid more attention to the advice of Mr. and Mrs. Pinkney, rather than that of Mr. and Mrs. Blair. Ah well, one can understand his position. They were his old friends, and he had met Mr. Pinkney only once. Not that one rejoices in having been proved right in such an unhappy situation. Still, perhaps it is some small comfort. I trust you will forget Sophy for the moment, go to this *soirée* for Mr. Falconbridge in your new gown and generally indulge yourself. I really think you deserve to do so.

In fact, put the girl from your mind, and turn your thoughts to happier things. I wish I could persuade you to come to Highbury for Christmas. I would come to you myself if I could, but you know how impossible it is for me to leave. There is always a small handful of girls who stay through the holidays, and then my three teachers will be away. Miss Prince has a brother who regularly invites them all for Christmas.

Louisa is improving, I am glad to say. But it is only just over a week since the accident. Yesterday Mrs. Pringle invited the girls to call on her and sent the carriage for them. It seemed a little soon. But Mr. Perry thought the airing would do Louisa's spirits good. For the first time since the fire, and well-wrapped up, she went out. William Pringle came, and insisted on lifting her in and out of the carriage and into Hartfield. (Not strictly necessary, I should have thought.) Mrs. Pringle was very kind, apparently. Made Louisa sit with her feet up on a sopha, and the young man was very solicitous. They spoke of Christmas. I believe they are hoping to have a house full over the holidays. Mrs. Pringle would not let the girls stay long, and Louisa was happy to come home and sit quietly in the parlour and contemplate the joys yet to come.

Well, dear Charlotte, look upon Sophy's letter as *good* news. At least she is no longer unhappy at school. Who knows, perhaps she is even happy, wherever she is.

Yours aff:ly,
Mary Goddard

Letter 62

(From Mrs. Pinkney to Mrs. Goddard)

Monday 9 December 1816

My dear Mary,

Sophy has been gone for nine days now. Captain Gordon writes that he inquired at the posting inn I told you of. It is near Bristol and the postmaster recalls a slim youth giving the letter to him. Captain Gordon asked if he was quite sure it was not a tall young man with an Irish accent. The postmaster said he was quite certain. He particularly remembered the boy, apparently, because his voice was not that of a man, and it is a remote office and not many strangers pass that way. Who this youth could be, one does not know. I suppose Sophy gave it to somebody to post for her. Captain Gordon says he is staying in Bristol and leaving no stone unturned. With this much, for now, we must be content. Well, I say to Mr. Pinkney, be grateful that at least she has written, she is safe, so she says, and now life must go on. Of course he does not see the affair in this light, and is still conscience-struck over the business, and worrying what he will say to her father if she is not found before the ship sails on

December 14th and he must send his letter.

Then during this past day or two we have been arguing. Rare, that we do so, I can tell you. The subject of our disagreement has been the *soirée* to honour Mr. Falconbridge.

Mr. Pinkney, though better, especially since we received the note from Sophy, is still not in a fit state to go out of an evening, being able only to hobble with a stick. He, however, has been insisting that I should go without him.

"What alone? And leave you! No, I cannot. I will not."

"But, my dear, you have a new gown, and you were so much looking forward to wearing it. Do you not want to show it to your friend Isabella?"

"That, my love, does not signify."

"But I think it does. Will the gown not be wasted, if you do not wear it?"

"You are quizzing me, sir!"

"I will not deny it."

"There will be other occasions," said I, uncertain quite what to make of him.

"Did you not tell me Mr. and Mrs. Knightley will be attending the affair?"

I acknowledged that they were. Much against his wishes, Mr. John Knightley had been obliged to accept the invitation. In the case of a man of Mr. Falconbridge's importance, not to do so would have looked singular, to say the least, and lessened the regard in which Mr. Knightley is held in professional circles. This was how Isabella had explained it to me.

"Well, my dear," continued Mr. Pinkney, "to *please me* (I was amused he should employ the very same phrase that Isabella had used to her husband) I should like you to attend. You can give my compliments and congratulations to Mr. Falconbridge. I should not like my old friend to think that neither I nor my wife cared enough to attend his special celebration. You will be going as my *envoy*, my dear. Now, if you will kindly ring the bell, I will send a note to Knightley myself asking him if they will be good enough to call and convey you thither."

Tuesday. All this happened *yesterday.* I kept my letter open as I was looking forward to giving you a detailed report of the occasion. It is now midnight, the party is over and I am so angry I cannot go to bed, but must sit down and attempt to compose, or perhaps I should say give *vent* to my feelings. Mr. Pinkney was sitting up waiting for me, and has been justly indignant and sympathetic. But now he has gone to bed. I cannot sleep and I require your commiseration, also, dear Mary.

The Knightleys came punctually at eight, and arrayed in my new gown and pelisse, I entered their carriage. Not unwillingly, I must confess. It was good of Mr. Pinkney so to arrange matters that in going I was doing *him* a favour. I saw through his little scheme, but honoured him for his unselfishness.

At the house in Berkeley Square where the reception was being held, a great multitude of carriages was drawing up to the door. Throngs of smartly dressed people were alighting and making their way inside. Of course this greatly displeased Mr. John Knightley. He had only agreed to attend with reluctance believing it to be a reception of the chosen few, and here was all London gathered. Rooms brilliant with candles, fresh flowers, an orchestra playing and innumerable powdered footmen— in short everything requisite to make a glittering occasion to delight most people and to deter Mr. J.K.

"Intolerable, my dear Isabella," said he, as we made our way up the staircase. "You told me it would not be a large party, and here is an insufferable crowd. The heat from these candles is beyond endurance."

"Very true, my love," said Isabella, fanning herself.

"We will pay our respects and leave," he declared.

We stood in a line to be presented to the guest of honour. I gave Mr. Pinkney's compliments, etc. but could not do more, there were people pressing behind us, and we had to move on.

"Do you not see anyone you know, my love?" inquired Isabella, as we mingled with the crowd of people constantly moving about and talking.

"None I choose to speak to," said Mr. J.K. "We have done our duty, let us go home, there is no occasion for us to stay."

Isabella must have caught my disappointment. She looked at me then said to her husband something to the effect that it might be deemed impolite for us to leave so soon. Knowing how difficult it is for her to oppose him in the smallest particular, I was aware that this was a sacrifice on my behalf. Seeing he was still determined on going, I observed that it would be almost impossible for us to depart while other guests were still arriving, owing to the difficulty of descending a staircase continually blocked with fresh guests coming up. Mr. J.K. was obliged to admit the truth of this observation, and we moved on to stroll or stand uncomfortably among strangers. In such a vast assemblage of people it was almost impossible to discover any acquaintance, even if they had been there to see.

Since Mr. John Knightley was not willing to make any civil gesture towards any of the people situated near us, Isabella and I were obliged, in order that we should not appear to be too conspicuously unsociable, to make artificial conversation to each other. We were industriously discussing the fine weather and what the chances might be for snow at Christmas, for the children did love snow, when who should come into view but Mr. and Mrs. Elton! They were strolling along with a stout, self-important-looking couple. Isabella exclaimed to her husband that here was someone we knew, and at that moment, Mr. Elton happening to look around and catching her eye, they had no choice but to approach. Seeing their intention, the stout couple promptly left. We ladies curtseyed and the gentlemen bowed.

"That was Sir Percival and Lady Lushley," Mrs. Elton informed Isabella, without any preliminary greeting. "I protest we would have introduced you, but Sir Percival knows almost everybody in the room, and they have many acquaintance to whom they are expected to speak." Well, thought I to myself, that puts us in our place.

"I think you have met Mrs. Pinkney," said Isabella to Mrs.

161

Elton, since she seemed bent on ignoring me.

"Indeed," said I, mustering my best manners in spite of my feelings. "My husband and I are members of Mr. Elton's congregation."

"Yes. How do you do?" said Mrs. Elton, coldly.

"Mrs. Pinkney has a Highbury connexion, also," continued Isabella. "Her sister, Mrs. Goddard, is mistress of the school."

"I have quite forgot about Highbury," said Mrs. Elton.

"Then perhaps you forget," said Mr. J. K. sharply, "that not only Mrs. Pinkney, but also Mrs. Knightley and myself have each of us a dear connexion there."

"Ah, yes," said Mrs. Elton, "Knightley and Emma."

I almost laughed, Mary, at the expression on Mr. John Knightley's face. Really, I thought he might have an apoplectic fit. But Mr. Elton, however, interposed with,

"Exactly so." Then, trying to make amends and behave like a gentleman, even if his wife did not act like a lady, he said, "I hope, sir, that Mr. and Mrs. Knightley are well-settled back into Donwell?"

"Very well, sir," said Mr. John Knightley shortly. Mr. Elton was obliged to turn to me.

"I hope, m'am, Mrs. Goddard is well?"

"Very well, indeed. And very much occupied by her school. You may be interested to hear that it is absolutely full. She has not space for one more girl." (I could not resist this, Mary, thinking of Mrs. Elton's comment to you about her own wretched child's education.)

"Mrs. Goddard's school has an excellent reputation," observed Mrs. Knightley.

"Yes," said I, determined not to let the subject drop, while despising myself for being so trivial. "She has pupils come from far and near. Her school is so highly regarded she has even two girls from India."

There was a pause. Mrs. Elton asked in a very unpleasant manner if Mr. Pinkney was well.

162

"Unfortunately he is indisposed this evening."

"Indeed?" said she in supercilious tones. "And you came out nonetheless? Alone? How intrepid of you! I should never venture without my lord and master."

Mr. J.K. saved me the trouble of replying to this impertinence.

"Mrs. Pinkney is not alone, Mrs. Elton. Furthermore, Mr. Pinkney particularly desired her to attend this evening. Mr. Falconbridge is a very old friend of his. They were in the same college at Oxford."

Needless to say I was grateful to him for rallying in my defence. For a moment Mrs. Elton was silenced, but only for a moment. In that moment Isabella attempted to speak.

"Mr. Falconbridge seems a delightful person—" she was beginning to say. But she was interrupted.

"Oh, you do not need to tell *me* about Falconbridge," said Mrs. Elton. "He is a very good acquaintance already. He came to church on Sunday. He is to be a member of our congregation."

"Then Mr. Pinkney can look forward to seeing him there," said I with outward civility. Though really, Mary, I admit this only to you, I felt extremely provoked. And if I had not been brought up to be a lady, I dare not answer for the consequences. But there was worse to come.

"I forgot to inquire about your niece, m'am?" she said suddenly to me.

"My niece, m'am? Do you know my niece, m'am?"

"Only by reputation, m'am."

I was pondering what this could mean and replied, "If you do not know her, m'am, I am surprised that you would inquire after her."

"All London is saying," she continued in a disdainful manner, "that she has run away with a footman. What a catch for her!" and she laughed affectedly.

"Pray, m'am, and how did all London hear such a thing?" cried I, goaded into betraying my vexation.

"Oh, I cannot remember who told me. Somebody or other I was speaking to. One meets so many people in my position. It is quite the talk of the town, I understand."

"Then the town cannot have much to talk about," said Mr. J.K. severely. "Come, Isabella, my dear, let us go into the refreshment room. I think you might like to sit down."

"By all means, my love," said she, giving me a sympathetic look, "the music is a little too loud in here."

Mr. J.K. offered us each an arm, for which I blessed him, and the three of us swept off without further ado. But Mrs. Elton had not done yet. A parting shot pursued us as we moved away.

"Madame Dubois is telling everyone how glad she is to be rid of the girl. From Barbadoes, I think. Is she not a quadroon?"

I affected not to hear, although you may imagine my feelings, Mary—seething with rage hardly begins to describe them! Even Mr. Knightley was so moved as to mutter something under his breath which I did not quite catch.

"Very true, my love," said Isabella, and to me she said, "dear Charlotte, I pray you do not let her distress you."

We walked towards the refreshment room. The Knightleys are too well-bred to belabour an unpleasantness. Instead, they commented on the music, the supper and the number of political figures present. But you may imagine, dear Mary, how my blood boiled. *She* certainly has it in for anybody evenly remotely connected with Highbury.

Of course, after that, I was not able to take any pleasure in an evening which had turned out so very differently from anything I had imagined. Soon afterwards Mr. John Knightley suggested that we leave. I was very glad to get home and pour it all out into Mr. Pinkney's sympathetic ear. And now I have poured it into yours.

Well, at least for a few hours, until I met Mrs. Elton, I was able to forget about Sophy.

Ever yours,
Charlotte

Letter 63

(From Mrs. Elton to Mrs. Suckling)

St. Stephen's Rectory
Arabella Street
11 December 1816

I protest, my dear Selina, I am positively haunted by Highbury.

Last evening, my *caro sposo* and I went to a reception for the new Member for Oxford University, a Mr. Falconbridge, who has joined our congregation.

Who should be there but Mr. and Mrs. John Knightley and that Pinkney woman. Alone, without her husband. Bold as brass. What genteel female, I ask you, would go to such an occasion by herself? She claimed Mr. Pinkney was indisposed, but my guess is that he was hiding his head in shame. Everybody is talking about his niece, from Barbadoes, who has run away with one Paddy O'Ryan, an Irish footman at the seminary where she was a pupil. It is one of the first in the town (one I would consider, by the way, for little Gussie when the time comes) and consequently quite mortifying for Madame Dubois, the gracious lady whose establishment it is.

This affair should take Mrs. P. down a peg or two. Imagine! A footman! But perhaps the girl feels more comfortable with that class of person. I believe she is a quadroon. Coming from Barbadoes, she is bound to be.

Now the barouche-landau is repaired, I wish you could arrange to visit us. But I fear Mr. Suckling may think it too late in the year to be pleasant. The roads will be dirty, but in your carriage with four horses I daresay you can conquer anything as long as James pays attention and gives a proper direction to the reins. How are your works in the garden progressing? I suppose it is getting too late in the year for that, also?

Yours affectionately,
Augusta Elton

Letter 64

(From Mrs. Goddard to Mrs. Pinkney)

Highbury
11 December 1816

Mrs. Elton! I am appalled! I did not think that even she would sink to such depths of malice and ill-manners.

My poor dear Charlotte, how well I can enter into your feelings of mortification and rage on the occasion. What can one say, except that to let such a person as Mrs. Elton upset and distress one is simply succumbing to her own evil intentions. Do try, my dear, to forget her and not to dwell on her spitefulness. Once again I reiterate. For the sake of your health it is not good to let such feelings overpower you.

How stalwart and loyal of you to defend my school! But really, it was not worth the trouble. The school, which has been flourishing, if I may say so, for twenty years, fortunately does not depend on the good opinion of Mrs. Elton for success.

So Captain Gordon is in Bristol. Does he suppose, then, that Sophy and the man are intending to go to Ireland? I hope he can discover something. It is indeed strange that a *boy* should post Sophy's letter. I wonder who he was? Well, at present all can only be speculation.

Now, to turn to other matters, I hate to trouble you, my dear Charlotte, but I have a worry I have been nursing for some time, and I would like to seek your advice. I am increasingly uneasy for the welfare of Miss Bates. I know I have spoken of her to you from time to time, and I have tried to convince myself that of course she is all right, surrounded by every comfort and living in a place luxurious beyond compare with her former quarters above the shop. But she has been gone nearly three months, and I feel it is very strange that she has communicated only once with her old friends here in Highbury.

It is so unlike her to be so reticent that I cannot help suspecting that she is dangerously unhappy. She may be living under the same roof as her beloved Jane. But Jane now has other objects of affection, far dearer than her aunt.

Enscombe Park! How does she occupy herself? Accustomed as she is to small rooms overlooking a busy street, to card parties and visits from friends, to being constantly employed with domestic matters, what can she find to do in a large country house fully staffed with servants? I suppose I am really speaking rhetorically, because I am convinced I know the answer. Nothing.

Her furniture, including her desk and the much treasured beaufet, are still in store at the Crown. I spoke to Mrs. Stokes the other day. She tells me that this new quarter's rent for the space was promptly paid in advance by Frank Churchill, and he gave no indication that any of it would be required in the near future. I know Miss Bates was very much attached to her possessions. Certainly she has not sent for them, for whatever reason one might guess: money, I imagine. One supposes she does not like to ask Jane and Frank for any, and the cost of transporting furniture to Yorkshire from Surry would be substantial. Of course she was whisked off so hurriedly she really had not time to consider anything, but I keep thinking how desolate it must be for her not even to have the comfort of her own things about her in her East Wing room.

I cannot get her out of my thoughts. Do you think my fears are groundless? Will you ask Mr. Pinkney for his opinion?

Your concerned sister,
Mary

Letter 65

(From Mrs. Suckling to Mrs. Elton)

Maple Grove
nr. Bristol
12 December 1816

My dear Augusta,

I hope you are not often obliged to consort with Mrs. Pinkney. She sounds a very odd woman. Out without her husband. Oh, fie! And her niece a quadroon! Run off with the footman! What a blot on the family escutcheon.

Amusing you should mention his being Irish, because a week ago we engaged just such a person to work in the garden. I said to Mr. Suckling, would it not be strange if this Paddy was the missing footman? Mr. S. pooh-poohed the idea, however, and pointed out that there must be hundreds of Irishmen roaming about England, no doubt many called Paddy, and this Irishman has not a quadroon girl, but a deaf and dumb boy with him.

I am sure you are wondering how this all came about. My works in the garden, as you call it, had come to a standstill when almost finished, through lack of adequate labourers. Extremely vexatious. I had particularly wanted the kitchen garden walls done by this autumn, so that in the spring Warwick could make an early planting and grow more vegetables than he has hitherto been able to do. It was quite fretting me that I could not find anyone to complete this simple manual work. Labourers are so rude, these days, and so demanding.

Then who should come to my rescue and supply me with help, but Mr. Suckling! Such an unlikely source! *Entre nous* I think he is trying to make amends for my disappointment over our visit to you, and his ill-temper on the occasion of the accident to the carriage. About a week ago an experienced seaman had applied at Mr. S.'s office to work his passage to Barbadoes. He had with him a delicate younger brother for whom he wished to pay as a regular passenger. Being a good man of business, Mr. S. saw that such a proposal would be quite advantageous. A ship was not sailing for ten days, and this Irishman seemed eager to work and in need of a place to stay. For some reason he did not choose to doss down in the usual sailors' lodgings: I suppose on account of his brother, of whom he seems very solicitous, and who might not fare well in the rough and tumble of such a place. The man was well-spoken and engaged Mr. Suckling's attention by his address. Very upstanding and respectful and claimed he could and would do anything in exchange for food and a roof over their heads until the ship sailed. Mr. S. asked him if he could lay bricks. The answer being in the affirmative, he engaged him. They sleep in the garden shed and eat meals in the kitchen. The man, Paddy, works well. During the past week the wall has been almost completed, and I believe that it will actually be finished at last. The brother, a slim youth with very short hair and ill-fitting clothes and always shivering, is supposedly his helper, carrying the bricks to him. I must say Paddy is astonishingly patient with this boy because his assistance is almost worthless. Still, I do not complain. I am getting my wall in exchange for a few candle ends and food that would otherwise be thrown away.

Yours affectionately,
Selina Suckling

169

Letter 66

(From Mrs. Pinkney to Mrs. Goddard)

12 December 1816

A note today from Captain Gordon from Bristol. He has discovered that on December 5th a tall Irishman was seen at the inn where he himself is now staying. (This is the same date that Sophy's letter was posted.) This Irishman had some meal or other there. Captain Gordon could not gather, or his informant did not know, if he had anybody with him. Of course that was a week ago and he has not been seen since. But Captain Gordon is encouraged. It leads him to believe he is looking in the right place, and he continues his inquiries.

Meantime, I have been keeping Mr. Pinkney company in his library where he is spending the morning composing a communication to Mr. Adams. This must go into the post today if it is to catch the ship sailing on Saturday. As you may imagine, it is costing him sore to write, and he is pondering and weighing his sentences with care, continually reading it out to me and asking for my opinion. Dear Mr. P. Sitting here surrounded by his Greek and Latin books, I would be amused, if it were not so serious a matter, that with all his scholarship and erudition he should be consulting *me* on the wording of this letter.

"What do you think of this as an opening?" says he to me. " *'My dear Brother, I fear I have some disturbing news to impart . . .'* "

"I think it may frighten him out of his wits," say I.

"But the next sentence allays those fears," says Mr. P., "well, to a degree. *'Before I alarm you unduly, let me assure you that Sophy is, as far as we know, quite safe and well.'* "

170

"That is slightly more reassuring," say I. "Still, he is going to be very distressed, is he not? It is a delicate matter to warn, but not unduly to alarm him."

"Precisely, but that we cannot avoid. There is nothing I can do to alleviate his consternation and at the same time to tell the truth. *'We do not precisely know her whereabouts, however, for she has run off with one of the servants from the school.'* "

"Had you better not say it was the footman? He may think that she is gone off with a female servant."

"I believe you are right, my dear."

In this snail-like manner, the letter, which was causing Mr. P. so much anguish of spirit, advanced slowly, taking up most of the morning, as you may imagine. But once he had completed the task, and Betty had brought in the chocolate, and we had drunk it, and he was somewhat recovered in his spirits, I broached the subject of Miss Bates.

You know, dear Mary, that I respect the intelligence and judgement of my husband in spite of his strange notions about Edward's safety—even when travelling in our own carriage. Mr. Pinkney says, he asks me to tell you he *regrets* to say, that he is perfectly convinced that Miss Bates is desperately unhappy at Enscombe. How could she be otherwise?

We discussed the matter thoroughly. You remember how long I resided in Yorkshire when I was married to Mr. Grenville, and that we were only ten miles from Enscombe. I recall the neighbourhood well. Although we did not visit the great families, we were well aware of their existence: their names, their titles, their country houses, each in its own park.

Mr. Pinkney declares it is impossible for Miss Bates to be comfortable amongst such people, even though they are her nearest and dearest relations. Nearest and dearest relations, as you know, Mary, though not with *us*, not in *our* family, can be infinitely less dear than old friends.

From *them*, from her lifelong friends, she has been torn away—at her age, and from the place where she was born. Besides, from what you say (to me a most extraordinary statement) she was the most popular woman in Highbury. Now she is nothing, nobody, exiled in remotest Yorkshire. Mr. Pinkney says what else could she be, but miserable?

He painted for me a vivid picture. Imagine, said he, Miss Bates at a dinner party at Enscombe. The long table, the servants, the candelabra, old Mr. Churchill, Frank, Jane and the great neighbours amongst whom they live, the conversation about hunting, shooting and the ordering of their properties. What is Miss Bates in such circumstances? Where does she fit in such a scene? She is a poor relation, an old maid, a dependent aunt, of whom they are probably ashamed, and whom everyone wishes out of the way. At Enscombe she has ease and abundance, but nothing else. Such luxury would make poor amends, in the opinion of Mr. P., for the affection of old friends by whom she is valued, and the happiness of unreserved conversation over a Highbury card table. In Highbury everybody was pleased to see her. In Yorkshire, you can be pretty sure nobody is.

As for her furniture, no doubt the Churchills do not consider her few bits and pieces worthy of installation at Enscombe. I never saw the famous beaufet, since I was never invited to visit (when I came, they were preparing for Jane Fairfax's wedding, remember?) but I recall your telling me she used to offer sweet cake from it to their visitors. What can she offer anyone now? Nothing. And if she is not valued and respected there, she has not even that comfort conversation among sympathizing friends.

I am sorry neither Mr. Pinkney nor I can be more sanguine about your friend, because really, like Sophy, what is to be done?

Yours aff.,
C. P.

Letter 67

Highbury
14 December 1816

Thank you for writing so fully about Miss Bates. You confirm what I have all along in my heart of hearts suspected. I have a plan, however, about which I will write to you later, when I have had time to formulate it in detail and have convinced myself as to its propriety.

I now hear from Mrs. Pringle that there is definitely to be a number of guests invited to stay at Hartfield over the holidays. Several of Mr. Pringle's Cambridge friends will be down again and they are talking of private theatricals. I am glad Louisa and Lavinia should have this to look forward to. If Louisa is not quite equal to taking a part, at least she can prompt, or at any rate be with other young people and join in the general merriment.

Mr. Rutherford will be very much of the party—when his duties at the church permit his being present. Mrs. Pringle consulted me as to what I thought about inviting Elizabeth Martin to join them, it being tacitly understood that Mr. Rutherford would welcome her inclusion. I solved the difficulty by saying I would ask her to stay here, since the school will be virtually empty, and I sent off a note to Elizabeth this morning. I made the excuse that it would be a great help to *me*, since my three teachers will be away, if she would come, as I need assistance with some younger children who are staying behind. Thus are the niceties observed! I very much doubt that I shall ask her to do anything except possibly take them for a walk in the morning if the weather is fine. I imagine, I *hope*, she will accept with alacrity.

I suppose you would call this matchmaking, dear Charlotte. I am almost fearful of breaking so fragile a bond by even mentioning the word, but Mr. Rutherford and Elizabeth do seem to be in a fair way to forming an attachment. They have been observed more than once on the river bank where Mr. Rutherford is purportedly fishing at this time of year. If they are every day together over the Christmas holidays I hope it will fix the matter. When I see Mr. Rutherford in church he looks a good deal less dejected than before. Someone actually heard him humming to himself as he walked through the village. A happy change, indeed, from his too obvious melancholy when he first arrived in Highbury.

Yours aff:ly,
M. Goddard

Letter 68

(From Mrs. Suckling to Mrs. Elton)

Maple Grove
nr. Bristol
15 December 1816

My dear Augusta,

I had to write again to tell you of a most extraordinary circumstance. I was right after all.

These last few days a Captain Gordon, formerly of the navy, has been haunting the shipping offices around Bristol, inquiring in all the boarding houses and doss houses if anyone had met up with a tall Irishman and a young girl. Eventually he came to Mr. Suckling's office, and the clerk, never very accommodating, told him he knew of no such people. Captain Gordon persisted, however.

"Are you absolutely certain that no such person, no tall Irishman, has booked passage for Barbadoes?"

At that moment Mr. Suckling came out of his inner office and overhearing the conversation was struck by the words *Irishman* and *Barbadoes*. He said:

"Such a person has been working as a brick-layer in Mrs. Suckling's garden. But I know nothing of any young woman, only his brother, a deaf and dumb boy."

"Deaf and dumb, eh?"

Mr. Suckling said Captain Gordon was quite struck. He told him he suspected this "boy" was really a girl. Then when he heard the details of their employment, and especially that this "brother" was always shivering with cold, he was convinced these were the people he was looking for. He asked Mr. Suckling if it was possible to see them.

"By all means, sir." And then Mr. Suckling, who on certain occasions can never resist a jest, inquired, "Are you a good swimmer?"

"I do not comprehend you, sir."

"You are a sailor, sir. Do you belong to the school of thought that considers it is better not to be able to swim and to drown quickly, or are you, as I asked, a good swimmer?"

"The relevance of your question escapes me," said Captain Gordon, who was not at all amused. "You trifle with me, sir."

"But if you are to catch them, sir, you will need to swim extremely well. The people you are looking for will by now be well past Land's End."

"In plain English, if you please, sir. What are you saying?"

"I am saying that they sailed for Barbadoes aboard the *Provender* yesterday noon," and Mr. Suckling enjoyed a hearty laugh while this Captain Gordon was obviously quite taken aback by the information.

"Did they, by God!" he cried. "Damme, I have missed them."

At first, so Mr. Suckling said, he seemed quite upset. But after a few minutes' reflection, he evidently thought perhaps it was not such a very bad thing after all, and declared, "Well, it is no more than I expected. At least we know now where she is."

"She?" said Mr. Suckling. "Who is *she?*"

So Captain Gordon explained the affair as you have told it to me, and himself asked Mr. S. for more particulars, and was informed how they had come to be at Maple Grove and how the Irishman said his "brother" was too delicate to be subjected to a regular seamen's lodging. I should think so! Even as it is, she must be an amazingly determined young woman to venture on such an escapade.

Well, dear Augusta, I imagine this news will create a stir, especially at the seminary and in the Pinkney household. I give you a present of the intelligence. Since it is *your* sister who employed them, you may quite feature yourself in the story.

By the way, you were mistaken. The girl, "the boy," is not a quadroon.

Yours aff.,
Selina Suckling

Letter 69

(From Mrs. Pinkney to Mrs. Goddard)

Hans Place
17 December 1816

Sophy is found! At the same time she is forever lost. A conundrum for you, Mary.

Captain Gordon arrived back from Bristol an hour ago. He

176

has been very perspicacious in the matter. He concluded that the young couple would try to get to Barbadoes. He has been scouting around Bristol for several days making inquiries. I believe he might have found them sooner, but they were not actually in Bristol, but at a place a few miles away called Maple Grove where Mr. and Mrs. Suckling had been employing them in their garden. Good God! As I write these words it suddenly occurs to me. Maple Grove! Mrs. Elton's sister! I despair. Am I never to be free of that woman?

Later: I had to stop for a while to compose myself. I now return to my narrative.

They have been living in a garden shed, biding their time only until they could embark for Barbadoes on one of Mr. Suckling's ships. The Irishman was to work his passage, and his deaf and dumb *brother* was to pay a few pounds (probably five!) for *his*. So it was in this disguise that she posted her letter! They sailed on the *Provender* three days ago from Bristol.

So, Sophy is gone. To endure such privation she must either be very much in love, or very determined to reach home. One can only presume that in spite of her boy's attire they have been living as man and wife. Whether she is with child, whether he will marry her, who is to say? If the ship does not founder in a winter gale she will be reunited with her father and her old black nurse, and can astonish them by producing a lover. I recall Sophy saying the man did not intend to spend his whole life as a footman. Well, he has taken a good step away from *that* occupation. I suppose he is a fortune-hunter and saw his chance, an heiress—or what he would deem an heiress, there being no son to inherit the plantation.

Poor Mr. Adams. He is in for a dire shock. Sophy, and Mr. Pinkney's letter announcing her flight, will arrive together on the same ship. It will be months before we can hear anything. Meanwhile, I tell Mr. Pinkney that it is best to put the whole unpleasant circumstance out of our minds. Brooding will serve no useful purpose.

Captain Gordon has now returned to Portsmouth. I am

177

sure the poor man is very glad to be going home at last. How does Louisa do?

Ever yours most affectionately,
Charlotte

P.S. I forgot to mention Elizabeth Martin. I am glad the attachment looks promising. You have told me yourself that you think the fittest destiny for any young woman is a husband. I hope you are looking about you for a prospective bridegroom for little Sukey. Only another seven years or so and she will be ripe for some young man. Mary, it is no use protesting. No matchmaker, indeed!

Letter 70

(From Captain Gordon to Mrs. Pinkney)

Mrs. Smith's Lodgings
Portsmouth
19 December 1816

My dear Mrs. Pinkney,

Now I am returned to Portsmouth, I write to thank you and your husband for your generous hospitality and all your good offices on my behalf.

In consequence of the pension I am now to receive, my daughter and I are looking for more agreeable lodgings. We seem to have found a charming small house with a view over the Solent. I believe we will be able to close with the owner in the next few days. It has an ample garden in which the children can play and in which I hope to occupy myself growing vegetables. It is *you* that has made this possible.

My grandson was pleased to see me, I am glad to say, though my granddaughter cried when I spoke to her. Children have such short memories. But *I* have not, my dear madam, and will long recollect your and Mr. Pinkney's kindness.

My daughter wishes to add to this letter.

Your sincere and grateful,
A. J. Gordon

My dear Mrs. Pinkney, I have the best news possible. Richard is coming home! He sent messages by a friend whose ship has newly arrived in Portsmouth from Africa. Richard's own ship is to be sent home for a refit and a change of crew. How I am counting the days until he can come. Won't he be surprised and delighted when he finds us in our charming new house with no leaking windows and badly closing doors. Affectionately, Charlotte.

Letter 71

(From Mrs. Goddard to Mrs. Pinkney)

Highbury
18 December 1816

I hope you will be able to convince yourself, my dear Charlotte, that this is the happiest solution.

From what you have said, Sophy will be content only in Barbadoes. Possibly Mr. Adams will now remain there, and if this Paddy O'Ryan is so determined on this course of action, conceivably he might make quite a good son-in-law. Evidently he is ambitious. That is not such a very bad thing, is it? In the spirit of this democratic age, which has already dawned in America, everybody, we are led to believe, considers himself the equal of everybody else. Perhaps with hard work and ability this Paddy O'Ryan will improve the plantation and be successful.

One must admire the young couple's ingenuity in planning their escape. It would appear that she is very fond of him, and really he of her, to effect it. She trusted him in putting herself in his hands—safe hands, she called them. After all, the enterprise was not easy to manage, and they must have put up with considerable hardship in travelling and finding their way to Bristol and arranging a passage to Barbadoes. One day I would like to hear how they contrived. It would be interesting to know where he took her to change into boys' clothes, and who cut off her hair. He must have known someone or gone somewhere to bring about this metamorphosis.

Well, well, Mr. Adams will now not be separated from his daughter and can settle down and watch his grandchildren grow up. I am making assumptions, of course, but it is a new world, my dear Charlotte. We must all be prepared for change. Revolutions have and are taking place. Consider, on a minor scale, the unusual circumstance of all Highbury being invited to Hartfield.

I really begin to feel Christmas is nearly here. John is getting out the trunks from the attics and the stables and nearly everyone is packing to go home. This morning Farmer Mitchell delivered to us two turkeys, a ham and a goose. Very plump and succulent, they look, too. They are hanging in the larder, and Sarah declares they are the best we have had in recent years and will be just ripe by Christmas. She and John, by the way, will marry and move into their cottage (within sight of the school) between Christmas and the New Year. I have promoted the senior kitchen maid to be assistant cook. At least she will do the breakfasts. This concession satisfies Sarah, and I am hopeful the new arrangement will prove workable. Meantime, I am mulling over Miss Bates's situation, and I believe I have come to a conclusion.

Louisa continues to improve. She was able to go with Lavinia the other day to watch the start of the hunt. The hounds were collected from their various homes around the village and together with six or eight men assembled on the common field. From there they set off on foot in pursuit of a hare.

My little girls have changed their skipping song with the season. Do you remember when we were children how we used to love to chant,

Christmas is coming
The geese are getting fat
Please to put a penny in the old man's hat
If you haven't got a penny
A sixpence will do
If you haven't got a sixpence
Then God bless you!

Indeed, my dear sister, God bless you.

M. Goddard

Letter 72

(From Mrs. Pinkney to Mrs. Goddard)

Hans Place
19 December 1816

Yes, dear Mary, since there is no reversing what has been done, the only alternative is to assure oneself that it is for the best. It was a hopeless case to make Sophy into a fine lady, and there was no remote possibility of her attracting a *gentleman* in marriage.

I suppose they will have as much chance as anybody else of being happy. Her father, once he is reconciled to her not playing the harp, I imagine will be glad to have her at home. I do not believe he ever could have contrived to retire to England. This O'Ryan may end up making a fortune in sugar and rum. Nowadays, money, rather than breeding, seems to count. At least far more so than it did when we were young. Rich people, lowly born, are making their way in society. I am thinking of Mrs. Elton's vulgar friends, Sir Percival and Lady Lushley.

So we are happy to take your advice and put Sophy out of our minds for the present, and are turning our thoughts to Christmas. I try to explain to Edward, but he is a little too young to understand precisely what it means.

Isabella sent a note round yesterday to say that they are departing for Highbury at once, a few days earlier than they had intended. There is a putrid sore throat and influenza abroad and Mr. Wingfield advised her to leave town immediately and remove the children from possible infection.

I have not mentioned this to Mr. Pinkney in case he takes it as a hint, or a *complaint*, that I would like to follow her example. Which in truth, I would. I confess I quite long for Highbury. After all the worry and upset we have had with Sophy, and to a lesser degree with Captain Gordon, I crave a change, and would dearly love to be with you. Perhaps if we had come, Mrs. Pringle might have invited us to the party at Hartfield. But it is no use talking of "might." Alas, it is not to be.

You must know how contented I am with Mr. P. and how grateful I am to him for his giving me, a penniless widow, a happy life and home. If he has opinions he holds dear, such as the hazard of taking a young child on the road, even if I deem them foolish, I must respect them. I will tease him, of course, but I would not pose a serious objection to his views by putting forward so strong an argument as the risk of influenza and therefore be seeming to dispute and question his judgement in order to procure my own wishes. Only the other day he remarked again how thankful he was we were staying home and not exposing little Edward to any danger. So you will have to dress your turkey and your goose and eat your plum puddings without us. Sad. It is too long since we saw each other, and I so wish to show you our beautiful Edward while he still is beautiful and before he becomes a great clumping hobbledehoy schoolboy. (Though in my heart of hearts, you know, I do not believe he ever could become like other boys.)

Adieu,
Charlotte

P.S. Mr. Pinkney has just come in from his club. We are aghast to discover, since it was her brother and sister who employed O'Ryan and Sophy, that Mrs. Elton is spreading the intelligence all over the town. Oh, my dear Mary, whatever does one do?

Letter 73

(From Mrs. Goddard to Mrs. Pinkney)

Highbury
20 December 1816

Maintain a dignified silence, my dear Charlotte. Remember what the poet said, a wonder lasts but nine days.

I do send you my sympathy, however, and wish I could comfort you in person. Still, much as I would love to see you, and disappointed as I am that you are not coming, I applaud your wise decision to say nothing to Mr. Pinkney. The regard in which he holds you is infinitely more precious and worthwhile than any number of visits to Highbury. You would not want to forfeit his esteem by even the *appearance* of disputation.

Meanwhile, here in Highbury, the young people are reading plays in preparation for the theatricals at Hartfield. When I say the young people, I mean, of course, Lavinia and Louisa, Mr. Pringle, Mr. Rutherford and Elizabeth. Yes, Elizabeth ac-

183

cepted my invitation, and since the girls have now gone for their Christmas holidays, she is installed in one of the bedrooms. Very happy and content she looks, too. Each morning I ask her to do some trifling duty or other with the five or six little girls who are left behind. In this way she does not feel under any obligation, and it all looks perfectly proper to anyone who might be speculating why she is here. The John Knightleys have arrived, I understand, and are settled in at Donwell. I dare say I shall receive my accustomary visit from Mrs. John Knightley one of these days. For Emma, I imagine it will be a Christmas composed of both pleasure and pain. Her first away from Hartfield. But the presence of her sister and the children one hopes will drive all sad memories from her head.

Now, I said I would write later about my plan for Miss Bates. Your and Mr. Pinkney's obviously sagacious and discerning views on the subject have helped me to arrive at a decision I have long had in contemplation. If any good comes of it, the credit must go to you, for shewing me so clearly what both inclination and friendship dictate.

Hetty Bates, as Mr. Pinkney says, is probably equally as miserable as Sophy, but unlike Sophy, it is not in her power to leave. Had she been younger, she might have become a governess. Unfortunately, like that of many another unmarried daughter, her lot has been to spend her best years in the care of her old mother.

Today, a chance meeting with Mrs. Weston in the High Street absolutely confirmed me in my proposed enterprise. Mrs. Weston said she had a letter from Jane who mentioned she was anxious about Miss Bates. She had not been her usual cheerful self lately, and was very quiet and thin. But when Jane proposed that she see their own apothecary at Enscombe, Miss Bates absolutely refused and assured them there was nothing the matter with her. Jane wished Mr. Perry were at hand to prescribe a tonic, as he had looked after Miss Bates for so long. I then confided in Mrs. Weston what I intended doing. She was very sympathetic, agreed with me, and said she would speak to Mr.

Weston. She felt sure he would allow the use of the carriage or help in any way he could.

I have accordingly written the enclosed. Like a proposal of marriage, it is not to be lightly entered into, for it is for life, and when I retire, I shall take her with me to my cottage. I made a rough draft, to be certain I phrased it exactly as I intended, because if what you say is true—and I am sure it is—her feelings must be very much bruised in having to admit, even if only to herself, that living with the beloved niece has not proved a success.

If you will excuse the untidiness of the writing, I am sending you this copy. I hope you approve of the plan.

Yours very affectionately,
Mary Goddard

Letter 74

(From Mrs. Goddard to Miss Bates)

Highbury
20 December 1816

My dear Hetty,

I often think of you in Yorkshire, and know what a satisfaction it must be to you to see Jane so well settled. But I hope you have not forgot your old friends in Highbury, where you are very much missed.

Life here has changed since you and I remember it in the old days when we used to go so happily to Hartfield to play quadrille. There is the loss of Mr. Woodhouse and your dear mother. Before that, the marriages of Emma Woodhouse and Harriet Smith and your niece Jane Fairfax brought other changes. Then came the departure of yourself and the Eltons. Now another family is living at Hartfield, and our vicar is young Mr. Charles Rutherford. One cannot expect time to stand still, and it does not. Yet much remains the same, and what I think of as the glory days of Highbury, when all the young people were courting and getting married, will surely live in our memories forever. Mrs. Cole, Mrs. Perry and I sometimes meet to play cards and your name is frequently invoked, with much regret, I may say, that you are no longer of the party.

Everything at the school goes on much as it has done over the years, except that this term I have more pupils than ever before. My three teachers really have more on their hands than they can manage. I am often, myself, called on to leave my regular duties and assist them. This brings me to what I am about to say. It happens that John and my cook—who are to be married immediately after Christmas—will move out of the school into a small cottage down the road. Thus with some little rearrangement, I find I can contrive a bedroom and a small sitting room on the side of the house. This has its own entrance.

I would like, my dear Hetty, to offer you this accommodation. If you would undertake the teaching of needlework, embroidery and knitting to the girls, it will leave Miss Nash, Miss Richardson and Miss Prince more time for regular instruction in other subjects, which they, and I, would welcome. If this arrangement would suit you, I would be happy if you would consider the school your permanent home. It would be a great pleasure to me to have the advantage of your company once again. Certainly Mrs. Perry and Mrs. Cole and all your old friends here would welcome your return to Highbury.

I know travel from Yorkshire is a consideration. But I was speaking to Mrs. Weston this morning and she tells me that Mr. Weston is contemplating a visit to Enscombe very soon to see his grandchildren. I confided in Mrs. Weston my proposal, and I have now heard from her that Mr. Weston declares that if you accept he would be most happy to bring you back in his carriage.

No doubt you would like to have your own things about you, and with your permission I will speak to Mrs. Stokes, and instruct John to fetch them from store at the Crown.

Ever your old friend,
Mary Goddard

Letter 75

(From Mrs. Pinkney to Mrs. Goddard)

Hans Place
21 December 1816

I have not the slightest doubt that Miss Bates will accept your offer and I think it very prudent of you to give her her own sitting room. You will have to make sure she stays in it.

No, dearest Mary, forgive me. I could not resist. She is your particular friend and of course I approve. I dare say she will be a considerable help around the school—though no doubt the girls will laugh at her behind her back. I am glad to think of you having a companion when you retire to your little cottage— whenever that may be.

Good Heavens! Mr. Pinkney has just come in from his club in a state of high alarm. He says everybody is talking of the in- fluenza that is sweeping the town and the number of people who are succumbing. He is vitally concerned for the precious Ed- ward. He says we must leave London at once, and do I suppose my sister would be willing to have us at Highbury? Lovely, airy, safe Highbury!

What a miraculous thing! How glad I am that I said noth- ing. I would not imperil his good opinion of me for the world. Now I know you are too generous, dear Mary, to be offended at this abrupt change of plan, and appearance of *expediency* in the sudden acceptance under such circumstances of your invitation. You know how much I have longed to come. How fortunate that you live in a school with so many spare rooms, now the holidays have started. Edward came running in while I was writing the above. I told him we are going to stay with Aunt Mary. He is practising saying, "Aunt Mawy," and finding it difficult.

Well, my dear! Who would have thought it? Betty has been sent to pack, and the carriage ordered for tomorrow morning at nine. We shall bring Betty and James with us. Within a few hours of your receiving this, we shall be with you. Oh joy!

Your excited and happy sister,
Charlotte

Envoi

Those persons who have been so gracious as to interest themselves in the foregoing correspondence, may wish to peruse the following collection of miscellaneous letters which passed through the post office in the course of the following year, 1817.

Letter A

(From Mr. Adams to Mr. Pinkney)

Barbadoes
21 February 1817

My dear Brother,

Sophy has now been safe at home a week. I wish I could have apprised you of this intelligence sooner, but there was no ship sailing for England until now. She tells me that you will be ignorant of many of the circumstances of her departure from the seminary, but of that more anon.

First, I hasten to enclose a draft on my London bank for £5.00, the sum you lent to my daughter and which paid for her passage on the ship hither. She has been most concerned that this should be promptly remitted. She confessed that she obtained the money from you somewhat under false pretences. She trusts she may be forgiven.

Second, I wish to acknowledge my error in not heeding your advice with regard to that egregious establishment of Madame Dubois. Mr. and Mrs. Blair, who, as you recall, recommended the place so wholeheartedly, were extremely distressed when they learned of the true state of affairs, and wondered that they could have been so deceived by appearances.

Apart from realizing that Sophy disliked the place, which seemed entirely natural under the circumstances, I had no notion that there was anything so seriously amiss. Cold, neglect, inadequate food. Of course I was quite unaware that she had actually run away and that you did not know her whereabouts.

So you may imagine my feelings when shortly after the *Provender* had anchored in the Bay last Tuesday, and I was sit-

191

ting on the verandah in the early evening admiring the sight of the rigging silhouetted against the sky, what should I perceive walking up the road towards me but two strangers, white, one, a tall young man, the other apparently a boy who seemed to be positively dancing with exuberance as they neared the house.

I was thunderstruck when the boy, running the last few yards, hurled himself at me crying, "Papa, Papa! Home at last!" It took me some few moments to gather my wits and to apprehend that this ragged urchin was none other than my own dear daughter.

Hearing the commotion, her old Negro nurse, whom Sophy has known since she was seven years old, and whom I continue to employ about the house, came running out onto the verandah and a very affecting reunion took place.

Meantime, the young man, ignored and unintroduced, stood quite at ease glancing about him at the house, the plantation, the view, good-humouredly waiting his turn for a share of attention.

It was old Mammy who, indicating him with a twitch of her head, and addressing me, said,

"Massa, he be gonna be yo' son?"

"My son!" I exclaimed in amazement.

"Oh yes, Papa," cried Sophy, and she took his hand and brought him forward. "This is Paddy."

"How do you do, sir," said he. I had to admit, in spite of my innate suspicion of the circumstances as they appeared to be, with a most charming smile and quite an air. "Is it too soon to ask for your daughter's hand in marriage?"

"Too soon, sir! I know nothing whatever about you! Not even your name."

"It's O'Ryan, sir."

"How came you to be with my daughter, pray?"

"Massa, by 'm by," said the old nurse. "Get washed up, now, Miss Sophy. You put on gown. Young lady no business in breeches."

"But breeches are very comfortable. I like them," said Sophy.

"Never yo' mind, yo' come with me."

The old nurse is used to being obeyed, and she hurried them off into the house without further ado. I was only too glad of some time alone to compose my feelings. Here had I been thinking I had a daughter safe in a young ladies' seminary in London, and suddenly I am confronted with a grubby creature disguised as a boy accompanied by an unknown suitor! It was enough to give any man pause.

In the meantime, while they were thus engaged, a servant arrived with the mail which had been brought ashore from the ship. Lo and behold, there was a letter from you announcing Sophy's disappearance. Oh, my dear brother, I do grieve for the anxiety and distress she caused you. I suppose until you receive this report from me you are even yet wondering where she is.

To return to the day of their arrival. An hour or so later, after they had been made presentable, they reappeared: Sophy in a white muslin gown and the man washed, shaved and dressed in an old shirt and breeches of mine, which I had discarded, and which Mammy had evidently salvaged. I asked if they were hungry, but all they would accept was some lime juice, Sophy declaring she was too happy and too excited to eat.

"Now," said I, "you have much to tell me."

"Indeed we have," said she. "Where shall we begin, Paddy? Will you tell Papa our adventures or shall I?"

In the event they spoke in turns, Sophy very prettily deferring to O'Ryan on all the important points of the tale.

Since I am sure you must be curious to know how she effected her escape from that "prison" (as she calls it), and as you certainly deserve, after all your care of her, to hear the particulars, I will recount their story as they told it to me. Incidentally, I suggested to Sophy that she should write to you herself, but she begged to be excused. She is not much of a hand at writing and in the week they have been here she has been much engaged with renewing old acquaintance and riding with O'Ryan about the island.

They told me they deliberately planned her flight from the school on a Sunday when she was to have come to you, and for which deception she begs your pardon. She believes you did not form a very favourable impression of her, and regrets that her misery at the school made her often rude and ungracious. She says you were very forebearing and she does not deserve your kindness.

On Sundays it was evidently the custom for the girls to be escorted by a teacher to church, the young ladies following two by two along the road behind her. It was the easiest thing in the world, said Sophy, for her to lag behind and at a particular spot, by pre-arrangement, to turn off. O'Ryan was waiting for her, and they dashed together through various back alleys to an inn owned by an acquaintance of his, an Irish publican. This man had a son, about Sophy's age and size. He gave up some of his son's clothes in exchange for Sophy's gown and bonnet, shoes and pelisse, which he intended to sell. Judging by the rags Sophy was wearing he certainly had the better part of the bargain. At this inn her hair was cut or hacked off, and some dirt rubbed into her face, and thus the disguise was complete.

Two days later, they arrived by waggon at Bristol, where they went to an inn for food. O'Ryan, according to Sophy, was always most solicitous to keep her under his protection. She was concerned that *you* would be worrying about her and was most anxious to allay your and Mrs. Pinkney's fears for, as she said, it seemed a poor way to repay your hospitality and your benefaction of £5.00. At this inn in Bristol they were able to purloin a sheet of paper, and later to beg the use of a pen and ink from a servant at Maple Grove.

Maple Grove was the estate of the owner of the ship on which they were to travel, a person called Suckling. O'Ryan had managed to persuade Mr. Suckling to give them work and shelter until they were due to embark.

They were glad enough of this refuge, where they were

perfectly sequestered from the prying eyes of anyone who might be searching for them. O'Ryan said he worked exceedingly hard to complete a brick wall left half-finished, as it was expedient to keep in the good graces of the shipowner. Sophy in her guise as a deaf and dumb boy was brick-layer's assistant! He said the people, these Sucklings, were not at all pleasant and had not been able to retain previous labourers. They were given very little to eat and apparently all but froze in the shed they occupied, only the coachman took pity and lent them a couple of horse blankets.

Eventually the day came when the ship sailed. Fortunately the captain proved a reasonable man, and since the ship was proceeding directly to Barbadoes their passage home was quite tolerable. (I shudder when I think how it might have been.) But such thoughts do not appear to have troubled the young couple. Once safely on board, Sophy felt she could drop the disguise of being deaf and dumb, and was simply treated as a rather immature boy by the officers with whom she ate her meals. O'Ryan worked his passage as a seaman, living in the fo'c'sle with the crew, so they saw little of each other on the voyage.

It appears that this person, this Paddy O'Ryan, will indeed become my son. Not quite what I had envisaged for Sophy, but evidently I must revise my ideas. He tells me he is an orphan, left Ireland when he was sixteen and has been making his way in the world ever since. He is now twenty-five and declares he is ready to settle and to work hard. He is penniless, of course, but they do seem to be exceedingly attached to one another, though perhaps the greater attachment is on Sophy's side. Mammy thinks highly of him, but then her view is not entirely disinterested since it is quite to her advantage to have them here, and she can bring up another generation of children even as she brought up Sophy. Well, I suppose matters could be worse. I see now that it was quite a fatuous scheme of mine, sending Sophy to England, and expecting her to play the harp. How one does delude oneself. She is happy here. This is her home. She wants no other.

To a fond father, you know, no young man is ever good enough for his daughter. I cannot begin to conceive what your sister, Sophy's dear mother, would say, but I confess the young man interests me. He begins already to see what might be done on the plantation, and with the greatest tact, for fear of giving offence or seeming to intrude, has actually made one or two useful suggestions. I suppose in due time he is likely to prove an asset to the property and to the family.

It is expedient that the wedding take place almost immediately. I suppose I must get used to calling him Paddy and resign myself to permanent exile on this island.

In truth, I am obliged to concede that ever since I came here there never has been a propitious time to leave for England, and no doubt there never will be.

I hope, my dear brother, even though it is unlikely that I shall ever see my native land again, that you will continue a correspondence which I very much value.

Yours, etc.

J. A. Adams

Letter B

(From Miss Nash to Miss Penelope Lane)

Mrs. Goddard's School,
Highbury
20 June 1817

My dear Penelope,

Doubtless you are anticipating the coming summer holidays as fervently as I am.

How it may be at *your* school I know not. Not many

schools, I believe, can be as generally pleasing as Mrs. Goddard's, but nonetheless I do find that however agreeable the girls and congenial the other teachers may be, one does grow excessively weary of looking at the same faces every day. One quite longs for a change of scene, of food and of conversation. I am eagerly looking forward to your company and the pleasure of our annual sojourn together at the seaside. How fortunate we are to have discovered our quiet little watering place and to have good Mrs. Greene's comfortable lodgings to occupy.

Little did I think, my dear Penelope, that I would be spending my life teaching school. When I was a girl I had great ideas of the man I would marry and the number of children I would have. To tell the truth I will not conceal from you that even as recently as three or four years ago I still entertained hopes of making a match. After all I had before me the example of Miss Taylor, something like sixteen years a governess with a family in Highbury, and yet she was still able to capture a most pleasant and eligible husband.

So, I thought to myself, why should I not have the same success? Especially as there was at that time living in Highbury a Mr. Elton, the vicar, unattached and evidently not relishing his single state. Although younger than me, that did not seem an insuperable obstacle. There were no other suitable females in Highbury except us three teachers here at the school. I blush to admit it, but I used to walk very frequently past the vicarage—I remember when he put up some new yellow curtains—and I also used every Sunday to write down the text from which he preached. I had some idea that this devotion would come to his attention and bear fruit. Alas, it never did. He found a wife elsewhere. Our present vicar, a young man newly come here, has recently married one of my former pupils, which makes me realize I must relinquish these foolish notions and resign myself to spinsterhood. All I hope is that when I am an impoverished old maid someone will take pity on me as Mrs. Goddard has done on Miss Bates.

But perhaps I have not mentioned her before? Miss Bates is an elderly lady whom Mrs. Goddard has invited to live here at the school. She is a former village worthy left penniless on the death of the aged mother she was caring for. (At least, my dear Penelope, we must be grateful that neither of us ever had *that* cross to bear!)

Miss Bates arrived in January. One of the Highbury gentlemen went up to Yorkshire to fetch her. (The very one, in fact, who was secured by Miss Taylor.) Since her mother's death Miss Bates had been living there with a niece and her rich husband, and it was not a congenial arrangement.

When Mrs. Goddard first apprised Miss Prince, Miss Richardson and myself of the proposal, we were quite concerned that Miss Bates, especially as she is a friend of Mrs. Goddard, might interfere or meddle with our accustomed practices in teaching and managing the girls. But I am happy to say our fears were groundless. She is a pleasant, good-humoured woman—whose only fault is a propensity to talk too much. Some of the girls mimic her and laugh at her behind her back, but they like her well enough. It is her province to instruct them in fine sewing, embroidery and needlework, at which she is rather skilled. It is a relief to the rest of us teachers not to have to trouble ourselves with these so-called accomplishments, which, although considered necessary for every gentlewoman to acquire, have no appeal for me. To sit and sew or crochet at pieces of fancy-work of no use or consequence has always seemed a most thorough-going waste of time.

Miss Bates has her own bedroom and sitting room and sometimes the village ladies come in to play cards with her of an evening. They often include Miss Prince, who enjoys a game. I must declare that the greatest goodwill appears to subsist between Mrs. Goddard and Miss Bates.

The former, of course, is much occupied with running the school and looking after her parlour boarders. At present she is arranging for the wedding of one of them, who will be married next week—at seventeen, if you please!

Well, my dear Penelope, we shall soon be sea-bathing. How I am counting the days.

Your sincere friend,
E. Nash

Letter C

(From Mrs. Ludgrove to Mrs. Pringle)

Upper Berkeley Street
London
27 June 1817

My dear Mrs. Pringle,

I thought everything went off charmingly—an occasion of great joy, was it not? Though I will confess to wiping away a tear. I suppose it is always so at a wedding—a time of separation as well as a time of union, in other words, an affair for both tears and smiles. The sight of Louisa and Lavinia walking up the aisle, the one attending on the other—so close as they have always been, now to be parted forever—quite overcame me. You will say I am overstating the case, of course. But you take my meaning. It is the end of their girlhood. That it has passed, and that I, their mother, have been separated from them for most of it, undoubtedly accounts for my melancholy. I must concede, however, that Lavinia does not appear to be grieving or envying her sister but is looking forward to living with us in London and the opportunities for society and balls that she expects to discover there.

But the wedding! Heaven knows it is not often that a marriage takes place from a *school*. I was disappointed. As you know, I had very much desired Louisa to be married in style from our new house in town. Mr. Ludgrove and I have so long been denied anything of that kind, that, selfishly, I had quite fancied a smart ceremony. But Louisa would not hear of it—*school* had been home to her for so many years she could not conceive of being married from any other place, and when William declared he would be wed only by his friend Charles Rutherford, and no other person, what could I do but acquiesce? I believe it gave great pleasure to good Mrs. Goddard. It was certainly a compliment to *her*, and having all the girls and teachers present made it quite a family occasion. In the event I have to own that I was wrong ever to oppose the idea of a Highbury wedding. London would not have suited near so well.

Already this evening by the late post we have had a note from Louisa ardently proclaiming her happiness and the virtues of your son. From the start Mr. Ludgrove and I observed that here were two young people who appeared really to *enjoy* each other's company, chattering away like two sparrows. My dear Mrs. Pringle, what more can one ask for in marriage?

I think it was *that* which made us agree to the match more readily than we had ever thought possible. I am quite ashamed when I think how coldly and formally we first received you. Perhaps you were not aware of our feelings? I most fervently hope not. If our resistance, I could almost say *hostility*, escaped your notice, it was entirely due to the advice of that excellent Mrs. Goddard. But since the wedding yesterday, however, I have been considering how quite dreadful it would be, now that we are so to speak *related*, if you had ever thought even for a *moment* that our objection was to *William*. I assure you, at our very first meeting I quite lost my heart to your son. May I be so bold as to claim that he is now *our* son, also?

In order to be quite easy in my mind, I would like to offer you this little explanation, which, if it is *not* necessary, I hope you will tolerate, and if it *is*, that you will understand and forgive.

Put yourself in our shoes, dear madam. Imagine, if you can, spending long, hot, wearisome years in India and conceive how we dreamed of a green and pleasant England and the thought that *one day* we would be reunited with our girls, *one day* we would take a house and be together again. Then, if your imagination is not too taxed with the effort, think of us sailing up the Thames in the *Bombay Castle* and, in spite of the cold January morning, our joy at first glimpsing the dome of St. Paul's. Home at last! But before we had even set foot upon the shore we were stunned by a letter from Mrs. Goddard. It arrived in a boat with the customs officers. Can you comprehend our consternation and astonishment as we learned first, of Louisa's accident, and *then* of her attachment to a young man only recently arrived in Highbury. And she but seventeen years of age! It was a shock we were not in the least prepared for. That Louisa, whom we had not seen since she was eleven years old, should be contemplating marriage was inconceivable. Here had we been rejoicing that at last we were about to *recover* our daughters, only to find that one of them was already as good as *lost* to us! Small comfort, indeed, to be told that neither Mrs. Goddard nor yourself would countenance any sort of understanding until Mr. Ludgrove could be informed and asked for his permission. We were only too well aware that his refusal would cause a rupture in the family—yet it was unthinkable that he should give his consent?

In such a state of anxiety and anguish we reached Highbury. Before we could confront Louisa, however, Mrs. Goddard came and took us aside in our rooms at the Crown. She most earnestly implored us to say as little as possible. Either the young people would tire of each other, or they would become even more mutually attached, in which case we might consider a wedding some time in the future. Discretion, delay and patience. Those were to be our watchwords.

It was good advice, and we took it. Our first meeting with our daughters was effected with much constraint on both sides. We were as strangers to one another. It is the price one pays in being absent so long abroad. Although in our *minds* we had allowed for the passage of time, we were scarcely prepared for the extraordinary transformation that we met with. The two impudent, clumsy schoolgirls we remembered had become pretty, vivacious young women. If the first quarter of an hour was awkward, it was not long before their natural liveliness overcame their reticence, and while Louisa talked eagerly of William, wanting us to call on you at Hartfield that very *minute*, Lavinia was happily explaining the recent theatricals and how the *whole* of Highbury had come to see the performance, *even* including the *Knightleys!*

Thus we learned that Hartfield and the Pringles was a household to be reckoned with. All pleasures apparently emanated from that hospitable and cheerful source.

But enough! I reprise our arrival, our first few days in England, only in order to stress, my dear madam, how rapidly our hearts were won over, not only by William, but also by his mother. We soon saw that Louisa, in spite of her extreme youth, was so excessively attached to your estimable son and he to her, that subject to a prudent delay, in which time Mr. Ludgrove and I could look for a suitable house and get settled, plans for the wedding should be encouraged to proceed. This, dear Madam, is the substance of the story, and I feel relieved to have unburdened myself. I would not want any misunderstanding between us. I hope to visit Highbury frequently in the future, especially when we may hope to enjoy our grandchildren together.

In fact, I am sure that what I am about to say next is not at all *comme il faut*. But having lived so long among *heathens*, I do not respect formality and decorum in certain matters as perhaps I should. Have you ever heard, dear Madam, of the mother of the bride writing to thank the mother of the groom for supplying such an excellent young man as husband to her daughter? If you have never heard of such a thing before, you have now.

Mr. Ludgrove joins me in sending our most affectionate regards, and I hope I may subscribe myself,

Your very sincere friend,
Laetitia Ludgrove

Letter D

(From Mrs. Goddard to Mrs. Pinkney)

Highbury
26 June 1817

Well, my dear Charlotte, the wedding is safely over, the bride people gone and the school once more restored to peace and order.

It is ten o'clock, and the last light of a long summer evening has finally drained from the sky. Now it is dark there might be some hope of the girls falling asleep. Until a few moments ago they were still murmuring to each other in their beds. The excitement of the day has been altogether overpowering. I fear some of the foolish creatures may be harbouring impossibly romantic dreams. Louisa's is not a good example. One cannot expect it ever to happen again that a wealthy young man, single and resident in Highbury, should choose his bride from among the pupils of this school. Oh dear, why am I telling you anything so inconsequential. I am very tired, and my head is in such a whirl I hardly know what I am saying. I do know that I shall certainly never sleep, so I have lit a candle and shall calm myself by writing. How I wish you both were here. We could have such a good chat together, like we did at Christmas, sitting over the fire with Mr. Pinkney while everyone else was busy rehearsing at Hartfield.

In fact I hold that play, *High Life Below Stairs*, entirely responsible for all subsequent events. It was those lengthy rehearsals that produced the engagements of William and Louisa, and Elizabeth Martin and Charles Rutherford. Not that I am repining. Far from it. As you know I positively encouraged Elizabeth, and it is pleasing to see so many blissful people about, their faces wreathed in smiles, and to know that one has had a hand in their happiness.

As anyone could have foretold, Louisa's wedding was a joyous affair. The parents were gracious, the young couple radiant and the guests behaved themselves. The entire school came to the church. Charles Rutherford performed the ceremony. With relish, I was going to say. Perhaps that is not quite the right word, but undoubtedly he enjoyed this particular clerical duty above any other at which he has had to officiate.

I think I mentioned how Mrs. Ludgrove had originally aspired to a London wedding from their house in Upper Berkeley Street, and although I was touched that Louisa should favour being married from school, it was not without some misgivings on my part. Sarah has been working for days to prepare the wedding breakfast. To feed so many, the cake alone had to be an enormous affair. I was afraid that John might be seriously put out at the long absences of his wife from their cottage, but fortunately he has always been partial to the twins—without being able to tell them apart—and was unexpectedly co-operative. The wedding required a deal of organization, most of which fell on my shoulders. Meanwhile the daily life of the school, lessons, contending with the various masters and their idiosyncracies had to be carried on as usual. Mrs. Ludgrove's chief contribution was to remove Louisa to London to buy wedding clothes! So even she was not here to help. Following the service this morning, nearly sixty of us sat down in the school dining room to ham and bacon, eggs, fresh hot rolls, newly churned butter, wedding cake and hot chocolate. It was a very festive occasion, and I am heartily glad it is now over.

This evening, Miss Bates, the three teachers and I had our own private celebration when we opened one of the bottles of fine Constantia wine kindly given me by Mr. and Mrs. Ludgrove. Did you know it is a wine that Napoleon fancied? And from South Africa, too, which is very strange. I presented a bottle to Sarah and John to take back to their cottage. Lord knows they deserve it. I see a light in their window now through the trees, and hope they are enjoying themselves. I have given them both a holiday tomorrow. The kitchen maids and I will manage the meals somehow.

William and Louisa left for Weymouth at noon, and shortly afterwards Mr. and Mrs. Ludgrove returned to town taking Lavinia with them. Is it not strange, my dear Charlotte, how outside forces operate to our advantage quite unperceived by us? Who could have foretold that Louisa's dreadful accident would prove to be an actual boon. It always concerned me that Louisa and Lavinia were so dependent upon each other, too much so. But the accident separated them. One had to sit upon the sopha, the other could still go out for walks. One had short hair, the other long. Now they could be told apart, which meant that everyone in the school could address them each by name without fear of being laughed at for making a mistake. The result was that Louisa and Lavinia became aware that they were not almost one person, and must do everything together, but two separate individuals each with her own life to live. Lavinia has already been invited to stay at Hartfield next month, but for the present she went off quite contentedly with her parents to London.

Ah, Hartfield. That reminds me. You were concerned that Mrs. Pringle might be planning to live with the young couple. Well, I am happy to tell you, that although I cannot imagine a more charming mother-in-law, Mrs. Pringle has found a suitable house in the neighborhood of Donwell, quite near the Martins. You are right, of course, my dear Charlotte, one cannot have two mistresses in one house, though what sort of "mistress" young Louisa will make at her tender age, I shudder to think. For the time being Mrs. Pringle is very unselfishly leaving her excellent housekeeper behind. Her whole conduct over the affair has been exemplary, particularly when one considers the short time she has herself been resident in Highbury, and how much she dotes upon her son. Upon my remarking on this to her, she was very good-humoured and philosophical. It was no more than she expected, bound to happen sooner or later, she was delighted with Louisa and wished them very happy, which, she declared with a smile, was the more likely to be the case, if the housekeeping and meals were well attended to.

Since I know you take an interest in Highbury affairs, especially as you met so many people at Christmas, I must tell you that the other young couple, Charles Rutherford and Elizabeth, are well settled in the vicarage. It is most fortuitous that the four young people are such good friends. I hear from Mrs. Martin that Elizabeth is already with child. So, once more, is Harriet, and rumour has it that Emma Knightley is also in the same way. And *you* tell me that Sophy is well advanced. I know what you think, my dear Charlotte. Too many babies. But you would not be without your beautiful boy, now would you?

It seems barely possible that yet another school year has passed by. Soon it will be the summer holidays, I confess I am far from averse to the prospect. To sit and do nothing will be a most agreeable change. For two weeks in August there will actually be no girls in the school. All those few who live here more or less permanently have been invited away elsewhere. Who knows, I may even be able to visit you in Arabella Street, especially now, since I can leave good Miss Bates in charge in my absence. It is some years since I was in London and I should very much like to see your house. Besides, your enchanting little Edward is at a stage when he is changing every day. My acquaintance with my nephew at Christmas only whets my appetite for more.

The candle is burning low, and I must try to sleep if ever I am to get up and do all that I must tomorrow. Good night, my dear.

Mary